FORBUSH AND THE PENGUINS

By a New Zealand author, a first novel of astonishing power and tenderness.

—Forbush, the young scientist, alone amid the penguin colonies of Antarctica

—Forbush, the clown, constructing a musical instrument of incredible complexity

—Forbush, protecting his beloved animals from a party of sightseers

—Forbush, racked by memories of a girl left behind in New Zealand

—Forbush, crazed by solitude, confused and horrified by the bloody cruelty of the living world

"Marvellous variety and excitement . . . suspense, humour . . . a really stunning book . . . tingling adventure . . . a haunting novel . . . fascinating"

BOOK PRESS

D0417962

FORBUSH
AND THE PENGUINS

GRAHAM BILLING

CORONET BOOKS
HODDER FAWCETT LTD.

Copyright © 1965 by Graham Billing

Coronet Books edition 1970

Printed in Great Britain for
Hodder Fawcett Ltd,
St. Paul's House, Warwick Lane,
London, E.C.4
by Hazell Watson & Viney Ltd,
Aylesbury, Bucks

ISBN 0 340 12514 4

FOR

LYNDSEY

FOREWORD

THIS is, I believe, the first serious novel to come out of Antarctica since man's new involvement with the continent began in the International Geophysical Year, and I present it with a certain diffidence. Not many of us have yet been privileged to visit the Antarctic mainland. It may be that those who have lived there will think they see in this book characters which they have known. My characters are imaginary. The only non-fictional characters in this book are the animals, Antarctica's original and only permanent citizens apart from the ghosts which haunt the Scott and Shackleton huts on Ross Island. At Cape Royds the ghosts have ceased to be bothersome since Antarctic Division built a special laboratory and living hut for the New Zealand and American scientists working there.

I could not have written the book without reference to the published findings of biologists who have studied Antarctic penguins, particularly those who have worked at Cape Royds. In a fictional way Forbush makes some of the findings which they have recorded. Apart from my own observations of Adélie penguin behaviour at Cape Royds and Cape Hallett. I am greatly indebted to the published work of Messrs. R. H. Taylor and E. C. Young who spent the 1959–60 breeding season at Cape Royds as biologists for the Antarctic Division, New Zealand Department of Scientific and Industrial Research; to Mr. Oliver Sutherland with whom I spent some time at Cape Royds in the 1962–3 season while he was stationed there as a research student for the University of Canterbury's Antarctic Biological Unit under Dr. Bernard Stonehouse; and to Mr. Brian Reid of the Wildlife Division, New Zealand Department of Internal Affairs, and formerly of Antarctic Division, D.S.I.R., who checked my text for scientific veracity. Dr. William J. Sladen's British Antarctic Survey report on *The Pygoscelid Penguins* was also a basic reference work.

I am also indebted to Dr. Vere-Jones, of Wellington, for a literal translation from the Russian basic to my version of the Mayakovsky poem quoted in Chapter 6.

Graham Billing

Wellington,
New Zealand
March 1964

CHAPTER ONE

WHEN the helicopter had gone and its sound was no more than a minute concussion of the air on his eardrums Forbush stood in the centre of the ring of stones to look up at the smoking mountain, Erebus, and ask for a safe conduct through the summer. In return he pledged truthfulness, the will to try. At once the ring of stones which still bore traces of yellow paint now faded and erased by the blowing snow and volcanic dust of Cape Royds blizzards seemed too safe to leave. In his sense of shock at the chill silence he imagined there was grass about his feet and the stones were cowpats or mushrooms. Silence. The black and white world which stood still was alive only because the smoke plume over Mount Erebus was curled and hunched and seemed to be billowing upwards.

The ring of stones marking the helicopter landing pad was on top of a small hill between Backdoor Bay and the Cape itself. Where is north, south, east and west, Forbush thought and carefully turned in a full circle as if he was a compass needle set spinning and, being too close to it, unable to find its Pole. Start with the mountain, Erebus, a giant, hunched and rumbling like its own sulphurous smoke cloud, towering broad shoulders, hard and undulant white flanks pressed over the frozen sea. Turn anti-clockwise past Mount Bird, a mere ice-mound beside the mountain, and lose your grip on the landscape as your eyes swing north, yes north, beyond Cape Bird across the frozen water.

As far as he could see the ice stretched off to the north, flat, harsh white, pale duck-egg blue where there were no snowdrifts, hummocked, pressured with blocks atilt and uplifted, rafted floes piled like broken grey slates against the island shore, against the angular cliffs of a trapped iceberg. There was no sign of water-sky, the blue-black cloud tint which tells of distant open sea, only the ice blink far north towards the winter range of seals and penguins, shining white, a silver lining to the Ross Sea's endless cyclone clouds.

"The ice is late," Forbush said aloud and found his voice thin and pointless among the echoless frozen rocks. The ice was late to break out and now the animals would be moving south undaunted, some doomed, across fifty, sixty perhaps even a hundred miles of frozen indifferent sea. The penguins would be shuffling in their six-inch strides across the uneven floes or tobogganing on their shining breasts, paddling over the snowdrifts or slick green ice, the skua gulls following, loath to leave open water and fishing, sailing high over the straggling columns, lines and divisions of penguins, wary for death and carrion; the seals would be slowly swimming from breathing hole to southward breathing hole, gnawing their exits from the sea. Their lives would end when their teeth were ground away. In the imperceptible spring life was moving south unquelled by the ice, moving only to the lengthening rhythm of the sun's horizon-round course, south into the blinding and timeless polar summer light.

Forbush looked west then across McMurdo Sound towards Granite Harbour, Cape Chocolate, Marble Point, Butter Point—at the coast named fifty years before by the proud men who came to conquer Antarctica. He savoured the names, rolling them round his mind, delighted with their familiarity. They were now names of his country, of a homeland, confirming his Antarctic citizenship. The Ferrar Glacier streamed full-gorged into the Sound and south of it Mount Lister topped the Royal Society Range in honour of English science; southwards still, Mount Discovery, bald-headed old man of a mountain with the evening sun burning orange on the snowfield beyond it and the icesheds of the Koetlitz Glacier, southwards yet past Minna Bluff, Black Island, White Island, the edge of the Ross Ice Shelf, the Great Ice Barrier.

Forbush was turning east again, eyes now on his beloved island, Ross Island, the explorers' home, Observation Hill, Castle Rock, the Hut Point Peninsula, the scattered sharp-peaked islets of Erebus Bay and the ice falls of the Erebus Glacier, the long sweep, nearer to him, of the Barne Glacier with the splendid, straight, seaward fall of its cliffs; the smoking mountain itself again. His feet, warm in the bulging wool and rubber bulk of his mukluks, ground soft and clumsy in the volcanic gravel.

Then he noticed the wind. It came quite suddenly and left him but it came with a sound he had never known before, a rustle, a whimper, a hardly repressed violence despite its slight pressure on his green and fawn windproof anarak and trousers. A spiral of dust curled about the ring of stones and subsided. Again the silence was complete so that there was only a small singing in his ears.

Forbush shivered. The warmth of the helicopter cabin had almost left his body and the cold began to sap his own reserves of energy so that he felt he was being diminished. He wriggled his toes deep in the wool of his mukluks and curled his fingers into the palms of his hands feeling the slight greasiness rubbed into his skin from his lambswool mitts. From the breast pocket pouch of his fur-trimmed anarak he took a pair of windproof mitts and drew them slowly over his hands.

About him on the ground were piled his possessions, his food, his warmth, his light, his ability to stay alive. All that in a small pile of flimsy boxes, canvas pack and kitbag. There was his field radio set through which he must keep regular schedules with Scott Base thirty immeasurably long miles away, a bulky package of padded green canvas bleached by sun, snow and blizzard. There were cans of paraffin fuel, a kitchen box containing his Primus stove, aluminium pot, pressure cooker, plates, mugs, cutlery, toilet paper for dish wiping, pot scrub, soap powder. There were four ration boxes each carefully packed with plastic bags of powdered, dehydrated or compressed food; a box with luxuries like jam, honey and sardines; a cardboard carton the Scott Base cook had stuffed with fresh meats, cans of strawberries and frozen assorted nuts; a box of books and stationery; a box of preserving chemicals, dissection instruments, a tin of paint, a leather-punch for branding penguin feet, bundles of numbered flipper bands, wooden stakes for marking nets. A net, binoculars, cameras; there was a big red canvas bed-roll containing an air bed, foam plastic sheet, heavy inner and outer eiderdown sleeping bags; a tent in a green canvas bag; two ice-axes, a climbing rope, a shovel, a set of crampons; and two cases of canned beer.

Forbush stirred his feet again in the gravel. It seemed that no time had passed.

"Well if that's all I have I'd better do something with it," he said aloud again and was again surprised. He stepped quickly out of the ring of stones, picked up first the heavy radio and walked, almost ran and scrambled with the scoria pebbles rolling under his feet, down the winding path to the hut. He had to stop again where the path ran out into a shallow gully in which the hut lay protected. But for the winter snowdrifts nothing seemed to have changed at all since last summer. The tins of bully beef, tripe and onions, oxtail stew, flour, biscuits, pickles, jams, pepper and spices, bottles of salt and sauces still sat in their neat rows along the southern wall. By the door, the two old sledges still leaned against the porch. Perhaps their timbers were worn a little thinner by the wind, perhaps another lashing or two had parted, frayed through by the gritty gales of winter. One couldn't tell. The dog kennel was still there with its pathetic rope's end still lying frayed beside. The hay bales were still there, pale yellow though their substance had turned icy and solid to its core. On a patch of bare ground grains of maize lay scattered among the scoria and grit. On the little peak in front and to the right of the hut the meteorological screen box stood bleached beside the flagpole's remnants. All the wood was bleached, dry, silvery grey and pale fawn, the grain standing out ridged and strong where the soft growth rings were eroded more deeply by the blizzard than the hard rings of winter in the land where trees grow.

"Go on," said Forbush and approached the hut with some sense of mystery, hardly wanting to intrude on the strangely preserved past. Walking through the snowdrift he stumbled over a lump of iron. He put the radio down again and knelt in the snow digging with his hands. He revealed an iron wheel still with some of its hard wooden rim. That was the remains of Shackleton's motor-car, the one which didn't go in 1908. That was all the remains of it that he could see but for the petrol cases and cans of grease stacked in the garage beside the hut.

"Damn. Here I am just off a helicopter, carting a radio down into this hut which looks as if it was built yesterday and I fall over a piece of Antarctica's first machine. A bloody motor-car, out there on that sea ice in 1908."

The mystery was gone. Forbush picked up the radio and crunched through the drift to the door of the hut.

Somehow the Cape Royds hut was imposing. When one stood in front of its door one felt that it towered up and seemed a match in endurance even for the smoking mountain itself. From above, on the hill by the helo pad, it had looked small and clinging rather pointlessly to the black rock and gravel, a victim of the snow. But from ten feet in front of the door where Forbush stopped to set down his radio, his communication with life and human warmth (it seemed to him, even then when he thought he was coming to terms already with being alone, that the radio was a symbol of his connection to the human race), the hut appeared to tower up. This was a friendly and reassuring thing. Forbush approached the door feeling under his anarak for his sheath knife. He had forgotten that the door was still secured from the winter snow and that he had brought a hammer for the special purpose of drawing off the nailed boards which held it firm. It seemed too far to go back to the top of the hill to fetch a hammer. There was an urgency again about wanting to go inside the hut.

Pressed against the weathered grey door and balanced uncertainly on the top wooden step he shoved the blade of his heavy knife between the door jamb and its securing board with clumsy mittened fingers, wondering how hard he could heave against the nails, and, it seemed, the weight of history which kept the door closed. His fingers clenched and he felt the strength of his heave on the haft and blade send a ripple of warmth through his shoulder muscles. That's energy, he thought, as he prised the squeaking nails, that's energy burning up, my fuel being used. Strange that one feels so clearly here the body's process, the weighing and balancing of life. The knife blade bent as if it would break but the board gave first and strained outwards. "Ugh," said Forbush, leaning his shoulder against the freed door and then his cheek against the rough scoured wood. "That's done it."

He turned the simple wooden catch and swung the door open. Dark. A dark short passage and another door. He jumped inside and strode along the passage, hit his head hard on a low beam and sagged against the inner door.

"Damn, damn, damn the fools, the damned fools—oh why didn't I remember," he thought as he clutched the door handle with one hand and rubbed his head with the other so that his woollen balaclava helmet scraped, it seemed noisily to his inner ear, on his hair. In 1908 the beam had supported a carbide gas cylinder for lighting the hut and had been a standing joke with Shackleton's men. He knew about it, almost as if he had lived out a winter in the squat little shelter. And yet he had forgotten. He felt one of them. He opened the inner door and peered into the dim interior smelling the cold smell of freezing metal and canvas, mouldering and frozen sleeping bags, sea boots, old clothes on which the sweat had stiffened with the cold, a hardly perceptible smell. He should have taken the outer shutters off the windows first but now that he was inside it seemed that he should savour first the feeling of the hut, the home, the winter haven. He remembered, as if he had been there, Shackleton's excited story of a 1908 night when, as the volcano's crater glowed faint red in the continuing dark the air was suddenly rent with the hiss of steam, the snow down on the saddle between Mount Bird and the volcano was split in a great hole, a fumerole which gushed steam and sulphur three hundred feet into the spring air and seemed terrible though it was miles distant. As he stepped into the square single room of the hut his mukluks made a soft thud and scuff on the wooden floor.

Slowly his eyes became used to the dimness. He could see the picture of King Edward and Queen Alexandra on the right wall, the manhauling sledge slung to the rafters beneath the peaked roof. What a heat trap, why hadn't they put a low ceiling in the place? To the right too was the dim shape of a door which led into Shackleton's room, the leader's retreat, reserved as his leader's right, peace and retirement from the smells, voices, laughter, ill temper of the dozen men with whom he shared the first winter. Broad-shouldered Shackleton, the great leader. This was his haven, his isolate heaven in the midst of his great achievement.

To his left Forbush saw a sort of alcove, another dim door set in a wall made of ration boxes named "British Antarctic Expedition 1906"; this was the photographic darkroom with its black curtain. In the alcove was a bench made of ration boxes piled on end and a table made of a teak door from some grand polar ship, now splattered with candle grease and stained with paraffin, the keyhole a blemish since it functioned now as a table and not a door. On the other side of the table was a large box with food, Forbush hoped, fuel, stores of various sorts, many comforting discoveries to be made when he was lonely later; it had been left by the biologists who paid a brief visit last summer. Against the left wall stood two large paraffin cooking stoves which might or might not work well, cupboards made of open ration boxes on their sides containing a jar of frozen Marmite, marmalade, sugar, packets of soup powder, an egg, half of a shrivelled lemon, an exhausted tube of toothpaste, half a paperback Western and the Penguin edition of Charles Doughty's *Arabia Deserta*. They must have left in a hurry last season. Fancy, a hen's egg.

Practical for a moment, Forbush reached up and unrolled the heavy canvas curtain strung on a wire across the alcove, dropped it so that it almost touched the floor. A piece of canvas, sail from the *Nimrod*, the *Aurora* perhaps, the *Discovery*, the *Terra Nova*, one of those foolish brave ships that dared to sail here in wood and canvas instead of steel and electricity. Now it was a curtain which would keep close to Forbush the warmth he created in his little alcove corner of the hut, a curtain sewn up clumsily fifty years ago with gangling stitches in copper wire, of all things, by some cold sailor, some lost and bitter explorer.

At the back of the hut, in front of him, stood the orange-rusted galley stove that once glowed red and warm in the night, topped by a black and sooty kettle, a large pot, a blue and white enamel pitcher, two wire grills for toast-making, and an ash rake. These he could see dimly and against the back wall the rows of tins and bottles, two frozen hams still in 1906 mutton-cloth on steel hooks and, at the left and right walls the bunks with the dim humped shapes of reindeer sleeping bags, frozen, the reindeer hair (each one hollow and heat-bearing, once warmed) still stiffly upon them. They looked almost, now, as if figures still lay huddled there, waiting to wake. Forbush knew this was an illusion and that the humped leather bags, blackened with the soot of seal blubber burned in the hut by castaways making warmth and food, still lay crumpled as they had been crumpled when the last heroes dragged their bodies from them and rose quaking in the cold morning to go on the last journey.

Forbush, who had forgotten that his head still throbbed, painfully remembered and rubbed hard so that his hair scraped warmly on his scalp again. On the stove also lay the Visitors' Book signed by everyone who visited Shackleton's hut—helicopter pilots of the icebreakers which crushed the way into McMurdo Sound at Christmas time; tourists whom the Americans brought for a picnic week on the ice each spring; sledging men from Scott Base running their dogs on training journeys before the start of summer field work in the Trans-Antarctic Range; biologists, zoologists, limnologists, geologists, lichenologists, glaciologists, geochemists, geophysicists, mammalologists; tired Scott Base maintenance staff on holiday.

"I must sign the Visitors' Book," thought Forbush. Then he thought that it might be a little silly since he was not visiting but making a home for five months and would, in fact, be host to all the new season's crop of bona fide visitors. He grinned to himself, ironically, he imagined, took the mitts off his right hand and unzipped his anarak pouch to find a pencil.

Date: October 16. *Name*: Richard John Forbush. *Address*: Scott Base, Antarctica (no), Christchurch, New Zealand (no), Citizen of the World and Scientist Extraordinary (hell no). Address? *Address*: Shackleton's Hut, Cape Royds, Antarctica. *Remarks*: Splendid (no), A beautiful day (no), Magnificent scenery (no), We bow our heads before the great men of the past (hell no), I.H.T.L.P. (I Hate This

Lousy Place—no—a barbarous Antarctic colloquialism). He left a blank and closed the book.

As he drew on his mitts again Forbush leaned against the rusty stove and squinted at the bright square of sunlight in the open doors. The hut became dark again and all he could see was the glare of evening snow-light, light on the rocks, on the yellow guano-stained penguin rookery area, on the faraway mountains. Richard John Forbush (yes, that was certainly his name), age 25, height six feet and one quarter of an inch, weight 11 st. 12 lb. on the inaccurate scales of the grubby Scott Base bathroom, chest 39 inches, hat size 6¾-inch in fashionable homburg, 7½-inch in polar cap to accommodate long hair, telephone number 73-299 (but nobody could ring him up), trouser inner leg length 32 inches, underpants 34-inch hip size, shirt collar 15 inches, single, life insurance far too high at £5000, inoculated against diphtheria, typhoid, tetanus and vaccinated against poliomyelitis and smallpox, blood group A, Rh positive, no holes in teeth, clear of sight, bronchial tubes soundly functioning though dry in the low Antarctic humidity, sex male, yes, quite painfully male.

Forbush took both his sets of mitts off again and groped in his anarak pocket for cigarettes. From a battered packet he selected one out of which not too much desiccated tobacco had fallen, lit it and spat out the dusty dry tobacco crumbs. He took off his woollen hat, felt the lump on his head among his still short hair and sighed. His chin itched under its growing beard so he scratched, thinking it was of reasonable shape, neither too round nor too pointed, not recessive nor lantern-jawed. But then it did not matter what he looked like, whether his eyes were blue or green or brown (they were light blue), whether he got pimples on his face from not washing frequently enough, whether he could talk or not talk, sing or not sing, whether or not his fingernails were dirty or his teeth furry. I suppose, he thought, that I will live very much as I would live anywhere else and keep as clean, as tidy, as efficient and well organised as I possibly can. His cigarette had gone out. There was no point in trying to light it because it tasted harsh and dry in the cold.

"What ho! There's work to be done," said Forbush in a

bold, loud voice and strode out of the hut immediately, up the hill to his pile of chattels. In five trips he had all his gear set in the gravel and scant snowdrift in front of the hut door. He wanted to leave it there because it looked practical and efficient like Shackleton's piles of unusued stores, but rejected this proposal after a brief mental dialogue and began to shift his cases noisily into the hut.

First he put the carton of frozen steaks, kidneys, bacon, liver, tripe, chicken and sweetbreads into the little cold store on the left of the passageway between the inner and the outer doors.

Inside he stowed his ration boxes and other equipment. He shifted some old cases beside the table and against the wall to make a bunk on which he inflated his air bed and spread out his sleeping bags. It still didn't seem right to take the shutters off the windows. He felt something of an interloper. Yet this did not prevent him from unpacking his personal possessions, the little concrete pieces of himself that always seemed to turn up in his baggage no matter how he chided himself for sentimentality. On the shelves on the south wall he placed a broken mirror, a comb, a hairbrush (pointless), a plaster figurine of the Venus of Willendorf, a toothbrush and a box of soap, a framed photograph of Barbara, a St. Christopher medal on a sweat-corroded chain, a cigar box of sentimental letters, a dried penguin's foot. "That's all I need," he said.

On the next shelf he placed his books. The poems of D. H. Lawrence, the first special Antarctic issue of the *New Zealand Journal of Geology and Geophysics*, Ivan Turgenev's *Torrents of Spring*, the Oxford Dictionary (pocket), William J. Sladen's *The Pygoscelid Penguins*, selected works from the metaphysical poets, fifteen assorted paperbacks chiefly concerned with detection and the wild west, and a treatise on animal physiology.

From the kitchen box he carefully unpacked his domestic goods and set them in ordered rows at the end of the table. After searching in the large chest he found a plastic bowl, a small plastic bucket, two tins of sardines, a can opener (this was fortunate since he had forgotten to pack one in his kitchen box), two grubby pieces of cloth which had once been tea towels and which he spread over his canvas curtain wire and, of all blessings, a large frying pan. He set the two paraffin stoves up on a bench beside the table and the two paraffin heaters on the floor one on each side of his living space to give himself a comforting feeling of being surrounded by warmth.

Obviously it was then time to take off the shutters. Quite calm and efficient, as he said he would be, Forbush took his hammer and went outside. Now he had a dwelling and it was time to reveal it to the world. It was midnight and the sun was hovering just below the western mountains so that the Cape rocks lay dark and shadowless and the drift snow shadowless white without depth or perspective. Already the hut seemed like home because he was making a brief excursion from its safety into a world which had changed quite suddenly with the lowering of the sun, which was not hostile but so indifferent that he could feel glad of the small corner on which he had impressed his self. Against the north wall he leaned on the hay bales and prised nails with his hammer until the first shutter was ready to be lifted free. This was done with ease, for the shrunken wood was loose within the window frame. Forbush lifted the shutter out and pressed his longish nose against the glass. He could see nothing but his own blurred image quickly frosted with the steam of his warm breath. He rested his forehead against the window pane, suddenly tired and feeling the sharp cold of the glass behind his eyes. This was no time to stop to be seduced by the blurred image of the uncertain reality he felt within himself. He went quickly round the four windows and freed them, working rapidly and with strength.

Then he took his shovel and an old ration box up behind the hut to dig blocks of snow from a compacted drift. This was his water supply which he laid in the passage between the inner and outer doors of the hut. Quite tiredly and unconcerned he thought of his radio and rummaged in the pack for its aerial wire. This he uncoiled in front of the door and then mounted to the roof, using one of the old sledges as a precarious ladder until he felt as if he was launched on wings on to the grey gables and straddled the steep pitch as if he were one with the now overcast sky that seemed to bear down on him, on the hut, the dark rocks and the frozen sea itself. He made the end of the aerial fast to one of the massive wire ropes which held down the hut against the blizzard, then scrambled down wanting to move quickly for fear of cold. The other end he made fast to a bamboo marker pole which he then carefully erected in a cairn of stones on the little hill beside the met screen. The first wind would blow it down. But now he had contact, he could talk, send a message out into that grey, indifferent sky. As he walked back to the hut door he had a strong sense that somebody was walking behind him. There must be somebody here, there must be somebody else, he thought. His throat muscles tightened slightly and he knew he was alone.

Inside again, behind the closed doors, he looked at his small inhabited corner. With the shutters off the hut was light, without mystery. "Somebody lives here," Forbush thought. "Why, it's me. These are all my belongings, all I have. First I must have heat." One by one he filled heaters, stoves and Primus with paraffin from a jerrycan, careful not to spill fuel for his own sake and for the safety of the hut. He began to whistle because the roar of the Primus was cheerful and because the snow melting over it in a battered aluminium pot appeared to be a manifestation of another life, something companionable which would soon bubble and add another sound to the silence. He pulled off his windproofs and mukluks and hung his woolly mukluk linings from a nail on the wall above the stoves so that they would dry out.

When he was sitting in his sleeping bag drinking his first cup of cocoa, thick and sweet with condensed milk, he remembered the rabbit and groped in his pack until he found it, a silly yellow rubber toy with floppy ears and lopsided grin. Forbush laughed. He remembered Barbara's voice and the mixture of question and laughter in her eyes when she gave him the rabbit and explained that he should introduce it to the penguins to see if their reaction indicated an intuitive knowledge of "rabbit" in the great communal penguin subconscious. "Anyway, he'll make you laugh and he'll sit anywhere you put him."

Forbush crawled out of his sleeping bag and sat the rabbit on his curtain wire so that its rubber legs straddled and gripped the canvas.

"How bloody stupid," he said and climbed into his sleeping bag to finish his cocoa. The rabbit swayed and grinned.

Forbush groped in his pack again, pulled out his clarinet in its worn brown leather case and laid it on the table, "Shall I play?" he wondered. It was one o'clock in the morning. Perhaps the penguins would begin to arrive to-morrow. He fingered the clarinet case with one hand while he sipped his cocoa, holding his other hand wrapped round the enamel mug for warmth. The hut was still cold for it would take hours to heat even his small alcove. He would not play, then.

Instead he climbed out of his sleeping bag again, took off his heavy tweed trousers and jersey and one pair of socks, turned off Primus heaters and stove, made a pillow of his discarded clothes, drew his sleeping bag over his head and went to sleep.

CHAPTER TWO

FORBUSH woke with a cold nose and heard the scratch and tinkle of ice crystals round the breathing hole he had left when he drew his sleeping bag tight round his head. By stretching his neck and tilting his head backwards he could see out. He peered, careful not to disturb the crystals in case they fell down about his skin. Dampened with his breathing and then frozen stiff the breathing hole looked like a kaleidoscope and he was aware of sunlight in the hut. To move will be difficult, he thought, and imagined the chill air on his skin when he would finally thrust his arms quickly outside the bag and sit upright. He wriggled his toes and swayed on the airbed to ease his stiff hip joints. Then he sat up.

Sunlight streamed warm and golden through the south windows so that he could see, through the gap in his curtain, Shackleton's vast iron stove glowing rusty as if with warmth. It was a good day and he was rising late with sticky eyelids. Half past nine was not good enough but then time meant very little when one was alone at Cape Royds. This had meaning only to the urgent feet of the penguins striding southwards towards him across the ice. He was sure they would be coming. This was Tuesday, 18 October and today or tomorrow, every year, the first penguins arrived at Cape Royds.

Forbush wriggled out of his sleeping bag rocking on his airbed until he could put his feet on the floor. He stood rubbing his arms under his woollen shirt and long woollen underwear, then his hips and his knees to remove the night's stiffness before dressing quickly in his pillowed clothes, rubbing his eyes and combing his hair with his hands. No water for washing. The pot on his Primus held a lump of ice. He sat on the large chest to draw on his mukluks, first the duffle linings, then the nylon and rubber outer boots which he laced up round his calves like *bundschuhe*.

"Today there might be penguins. I will make preparations all day and tonight I will set up the radio and talk to base and then I will read Ivan Turgenev—no, not Turgenev because that book is about love, which must be distressing—but I will read, drink cocoa and go to bed early because if the penguins don't come today they will surely come tomorrow."

Forbush was surprised at this long and formal speech, smiled self-consciously and decided he had better make a policy decision about talking aloud. His voice always caught him unawares as if another person was making the sound. "I need noise," he said loudly and firmly and the words rattled on his eardrums, echoing in his dry throat and lungs. He went outside hatless and with bare hands to look at the day and perform its first peaceful function.

The sky was utterly blue and clear. A slight wind blew down the gully from behind the hut as if the mountain breathed on him and he felt its strength and influence. The smoke plume was blown out wispy and straight today, a sulphurous yellow band across the sky at 13,000 feet like a stage above which danced the sun. His ears began to sting and he felt the sharp pain of cold in his finger-tips. The wind ruffled his hair and laid cold hands on his scalp.

Forbush shivered and thrust his hands deep into his pockets standing hunched, his knees close together, elbows pressed close to his body. He wrinkled his nose feeling the cold prickling on his nostrils as if little needles of ice were embedding themselves in his flesh. The Cape was timeless and quiet with a complete absence of sound he had never known before, even in the high country of home where crickets always sing out the summer among the tussock, or the tussocks whisper with wind, or twigs crack as deer move in the night bush, or the mountain faces groan and creak with an imminent avalanche.

The world was dead but for the shadows moving imperceptibly round hut, stones and expedition wreckage. The penguin rookery was a mere yellow stain across the Cape rocks beyond frozen Pony Lake and the western mountains were a pale grey frieze almost lost in the cold Antarctic haze forty miles away across McMurdo Sound. Forbush shuffled back into his hut to light his heaters, stoves and the Primus and cook a warming breakfast of porridge, bacon, and coffee. He carefully rationed himself to two slices of bread from the three loaves spared him by the Scott Base cook.

As he melted a final pot of snow for dish-washing he took out his papers, the rough notes covering a day's reconnaissance visit to the rookery last season, maps on which he would plot the positions of the small colonies into which the rookery was divided, lists of band numbers for birds marked in previous brief visits by other biologists, his directive from the Superintendent of the Antarctic Division, Department of Scientific and Industrial Research.

Directive to R. F. Forbush, Cape Royds Biological Expedition.

"On arrival at Scott Base you will prepare field stores and biological equipment sufficient to support yourself and your research work for a period of up to five months. The Leader, Scott Base, will arrange for you to be set down at Cape Royds by United States Navy helicopter about 16 October and you should make every endeavour to have all your equipment ready to meet this date. At Cape Royds you will live in Shackleton's hut built for the British Antarctic Expedition 1907–09. While living in the hut you will ensure that it is not damaged or affected in any way by your residence since it is a historic monument of considerable importance on the Antarctic continent. By virtue of your residence there you will also act as custodian of the hut and ensure that no visitors of any nation damage it in any way or remove any souvenirs of their visit."

Forbush put the paper down and shook some soap powder into the now warm pot of dish-water. He carefully cleaned his dishes and dried them with toilet paper, making a resolution to cleanse the tattered tea towels. "Custodian of this place. Think of it. I'm living in a bloody monument." As he wiped down the teak table he scrubbed a little harder at the grease spots.

"While you must be prepared to spend a considerable part of the season alone and to function as an independent unit of the summer programme it may be possible to provide you with an assistant from time to time throughout the season."

"People. Hell, who wants people?" Forbush said as he put on his eiderdown jacket and seated himself on his bed leaning his elbows on the table. The air was still chill. "Anyway, come Christmas Starshot will be glad to get away from base for a while." He thought warmly of Bill Starshot (William Samuel), companion of a past summer on the ice and of many summers in the hills of home, Starshot the surveyor, the map maker, with his passion for knowing exactly where he stood, for marking, delineating, recording, curious Starshot who was only lately becoming aware of the lack of bearings in his own mind.

"The aim of your expedition will be to make the first detailed population study of the Adélie penguin rookery at Cape Royds from the time of the arrival of the first birds (according to previous observers, 18–19 October), to provide detailed maps of the rookery area and the colonies within the rookery, to mark suitable nest sites so that they may be used as control areas for observations in later seasons, to record use of a small number of previously marked sites, to band a selected group of adult birds and chicks and experiment with any other methods of penguin marking and banding which you think suitable. You will also make an estimate of the McCormick Skua population at Cape Royds paying particular attention to the skuas which prey directly on penguin eggs and chicks in the rookery. If possible you should also attempt to capture and band skua chicks and adults.

"Since Cape Royds is the world's southernmost penguin colony you should pay particular attention to causes of mortality in the rookery whether from predating skuas or climatic factors exaggerated at this the southern limit of the Adélie penguin range."

"The pompous old goat," said Forbush. He had written

the first draft of the directive himself but as always the Superintendent had turned it into the cumbersome language of Government. Forbush took a fork and scratched his back casually, hoping that he would soon be so dirty his skin would not bother to itch.

"If possible and depending on the amount of time available to you after you have allowed for regular counts of breeding birds, eggs, chicks, non-breeding wanderers and yearlings, and regular daily observation periods which will contribute data on breeding behaviour, you should direct your attention to special studies of penguin physiology.

"This will involve killing for dissection but since the stability of the rookery population is thought to be doubtful you should severely limit the number of birds taken for dissection. This work should be in the nature of a pilot study with particular reference to blood supply to the limbs, and thickness of blubber layers and condition of reproductory organs of breeding birds at various times during courtship, egg incubation and chick rearing.

"You should also collect whenever possible specimens of mites, ticks, and any other parasites found on birds and attempt to assess whether these inhabit their hosts only during the breeding period at the rookery or remain with the birds at sea.

"Since there is evidence that the rookery population is slowly declining and that the presence of men, dogs, aircraft and vehicles in the McMurdo Sound area may be a factor in this decline you should make every effort to see that visitors to the rookery area do not cause disturbance to sitting birds.

"Throughout the time of your expedition you will be under the full authority and control of the Leader, Scott Base. You will arrange regular radio schedule times for contact with the base and maintain them without fail. You will remember at all times that you must take no risks and confine your travel to the rookery and its environs.

"As soon as possible after your return to New Zealand (you should not leave the rookery until the last bird has departed for its winter range at sea) you will furnish a

26

report to the Superintendent, Antarctic Division, out-lining the conduct of the operation and summarising your findings."

At the end of the document was a handwritten message. "You've got a tough job Dick—Good Luck." And the Super-intendent's signature.

Forbush wiped his running nose and wished it was time to open a can of beer. Not until the sun's over the yardarm. He felt tired and cold, his limbs heavy. No penguins yet. He had not even begun and five months seemed as long as the earth would ever exist. He stood up and immediately felt warmer because warmer air was slowly filling the hut, spreading downwards from the ceiling.

"I must go out," he thought. "I must go out. I must see if they are coming." Today was the day, today or tomorrow. He would have company. He would have noise, smells, mov-ing creatures about him. The Cape would be alive, stirring, its earth viable, its ice inhabited. He began the tedious and endless task of putting on clothes—trousers, anarak, woollen hat pulled down over his ears, lambswool mitts, windproof mitts, chocolate, cigarettes, matches, pocket-knife and piece of cord in the anarak pocket, snow goggles. These clothes always made him feel clumsy and cut off from the normal visual and tactile sense of the surrounding world. He slung binoculars over his shoulder, picked up his ice-axe and left the hut.

He ran quickly across the heavy and deep snowdrift be-tween the hut and Pony Lake, careful not to slide on its frozen crust, and then across the lake itself slowing down where the blue ice was bare of snow and its surface slick with the meagre heat of the sun. There was a special way of running across blue lake or glacier ice always treach-erous and slippery at noon—a slightly hunched and loose-shouldered stance with a stiff-legged stride or rather a rapid sliding forward of the flat-soled mukluks, like a fly run-ning up a window pane.

Across the lake Forbush trotted on through the shallow saddle which gave access to the sea between Flagstaff Hill and the northern slopes of the rookery. Guano and scattered nest pebbles were under his feet. He turned away from the rookery beach and climbed moving south on to the Cape itself to perch among the frost-weathered lava boulders above its one-hundred-foot cliff. Here, he could see north and south up and down the Sound, west to the mountains and east towards the towering volcano. Sheltered from the wind and aglow with sunlight he imagined he could hear crickets singing and wondered when his ears would give up the pretence. Then he realised that that noise was real and far out over the ice he saw a Hercules transport plane gliding in on its letdown to Williams Field, the McMurdo Sound airport. All the way from New Zealand, home, 2200 miles in the warm north. There were no penguins.

Forbush took his binoculars from their case and scanned northwards over the sea ice still expecting to see the bobbing black shapes of the first birds stumbling their way towards their summer home, their brief weeks of ecstasy, their harsh and necessary love affairs and their patient labours of parenthood. The ice was bare of life, pale green and blue, remote and white, coloured with the sterile hues of air and water. The iceberg stranded to the north near Cape Bird was like a castle keep, an outpost in the great ice wall, a sentinel with a mission against life.

Forbush huddled the rocks, crouched with his thighs drawn up to his chest in a heat-conserving ball and rested the binoculars on his knees while he pulled up his anarak hood against a cold breath from the mountain.

"I wonder how far out the ice edge is, how far away the open sea can lie," he said silently though moving his lips to stretch them against the stiffening cold. How far do the penguins have to come anyway? How far north must they go for the winter? Is it right to the pack-ice edge above the Antarctic Circle? Do they spend the whole winter at sea north of the ice and swim hundreds of miles south each spring? How do they live in winter, through the dark patient months until their gonads swell and tighten again to the rhythm of the southward moving sun, driving them blindly and instinctively southwards to the land?

Was there any real difference between the way in which the sun imposed a rhythm on the lives of the penguins and

28

the way the moon caused the huge swell and ebb of tidal oceans? All round the Antarctic continent millions of animals were now moving south as if drawn by some immeasurable tidal force so that, in their millions, their kind would continue year by year—an individual was a meaningless entity, an insignificant portion of the animal tide. Forbush was appalled and felt suddenly as if he, himself, was trapped in the tide of moving south, of moving north, of being born, living, growing and inconsequentially dying. And could life really end if its material instantly became part of another life—the life in the egg yolk the skua gull carefully sipped became part of the skua gull, and the excreta of the skua gull became food for the scaly lichens which clung to the Cape rocks or the algae which bloomed when Pony Lake thawed in summer.

Even the freezing of the sea helped to regulate the animal tide, for it released cold salt-heavy water which played its motivating part in the endless circulation of the Southern Ocean so that the sea was continually and richly replenished by nutrient chemicals, with vegetable plankton forming and using the endless summer sunlight to generate almost infinite quantities of itself, like the endless generation of grasslands across North America, Europe and Asia. And in the vast vegetable seas the whalefeed, the shrimp-like krill, multiplied in geometric progression. And on the krill fed fish, and the penguins and flying birds fed on fish and krill, and the seals fed on fish and krill and penguins, and the giant whales tending their circumpolar pastures rolled ceaselessly among the endless west-wind driven storms and swells opening and closing their cavernous jaws to suck in the oceans thick with krill and eat their fill and breed and suckle their monstrous calves from monstrous breasts rich with the milk of the Mother of Waters.

Out under the ice of McMurdo Sound the cycle was beginning again. Soon the ice would groan and crack. Already its under-surface would be growing pitted and rotten with the warmer spring waters. In the end the sea would split and open and the floes float away to the north. There would be the sound of waves breaking on the shore of Access Beach, a sound which Forbush could not remember. He could merely see visions, as he huddled against the black rocks, of a golden beach, hot sand and breaking Pacific swells.

"How far out is the ice edge, the open water?" Ten, fifteen miles, it surely couldn't be any more. Daily, the floes would be splitting and parting from the northern edge, floating north into the Ross Sea, up the coast of Victoria Land and west round Cape Adare four hundred miles away. Beneath the cliffs, almost at his feet, the ice looked so solid and permanent. No penguins, not a sight, no life yet.

Forbush got to his feet and walked slowly down to the beach among the rocks. The water-worn gravel and boulders were covered with a thin layer of drift and, near water level, with ice. On to this he stepped until he came to the hinge crack which allowed the floating sea ice to move a few inches each day in response to the dull tides of the Sound. The crack gaped a foot wide and he looked down into the strange blue and violet depths and its walls dusted with dense white ice crystals. He probed the far edge with his ice-axe to test its safety, stepped across and walked thirty yards to a stranded growler, a jagged piece of heavy sea ice like a miniature iceberg. The ice was a milky colour with a velvety sheen under his feet.

From here the hut was out of sight and he could see only the rookery slopes, the Cape and the mountain's smoking summit. Without the reflected warmth from the rocks the air was much colder. Forbush became aware that the air was filled with minute falling ice crystals which were now imparting a delicate bloom of frost to his green anarak, settling quite thickly in the seams and creases. He could not feel them fall on his face or detect their movement but slowly they gathered on his body. He turned towards the sun now swinging lower west of Mount Bird and the scallop-shell shape of Beaufort Island dimly rising forty miles north. The ice crystals, each one a minute dancing prism, formed themselves into a round rainbow encircling the sun as he looked, and as the thickness of their shower ebbed and flowed four dog-suns appeared at the rainbow's quadrant points. It seemed as though a universe was being created, destroyed and recreated before his eyes, exquisitely controlled by the laws of light, as if he was observing a cold and holy act of physical creation which irradiated his whole being. He gazed until the sun's rays pierced his eyes like sharp knives and then turned blind and stumbling for the shore abandoned and alone.

He did not stop until he stood in the centre of the rookery sheltered again from the harsh ice light, his eyes watering and blinking as he rubbed them with the thumb and forefinger of a bared hand. Slowly he could see again. The yellow guano stain of the rookery stretched a hundred yards to the south and fifty yards to the north. He thought he could determine the limits of each small colony within the area from the pattern of nest mounds—slight hummocks built up by decades, perhaps even centuries of guano deposition, each with a shallow scraped depression. Around them lay the raw material of nest building. Stones. Small jagged pebbles blown from the mounds by winter storms and scattered by the scuttling crowds of last summer's fledglings. Just cold, hard stones and yet they are the penguins' secret of life, Forbush thought.

At his feet lay the twisted and desiccated body of a dead chick, dried, shrunken and yellowed with gaping beak and eye sockets which seemed to give its head expression. Flippers and short legs were spread out and yet retaining some of their scaly skin and feathers. Forbush looked at the ground around him and saw other bodies, bones, pieces of bone, flippers, feet, heads, vertebrae, some lying loose on the surface, others half buried in guano and the mud of a summer's thaw, animal wreckage and organic refuse, all shrivelled in the Antarctic drought. He stirred the skeleton with his foot, felt suddenly indifferent and then hungry. With a last look seawards he walked slowly on towards the hut.

In the middle of the lake he looked down into the clear blue ice and wondered how the frost could possibly form such perfect patterns of ferns and flowers, rosettes and sprays and contain them pristine and exquisite etched deep within the substance of the ice. He jumped hard and stiff-kneed up and down on the ice knowing it would have no effect and that the simple inhuman loveliness of the patterns would remain. He stood still and stared down again until the physical world embraced him and seemed to encase him in its immutable and frozen regulations, to draw him, soulless, into the subtle chemistry of the sun.

The hut was warm by the time he returned and the pleasure of feeling warm air on his face so intense that he felt immediately removed and shut off from the world outside. He made a quick excursion to get snow for water and brewed coffee while he cut thick slices of bread and canned corned beef for lunch. At eight o'clock he could use the radio and talk to base.

Until then he would lie on his bed and read. He would get up every hour and look at the rookery to see if any birds had arrived. By half past seven the mountain glaciers across the Sound were burning orange in the low sun and the frost haze was like smoke among them. The rookery was silent.

In the passage between the hut doors Forbush unpacked his radio, leaving the outer door open after he had connected the aerial. The minutes dragged. He lit a cigarette and sat on the doorstep sheltered from the wind and hardly cold. Alex Fisher the radio operator would be walking into the radio room and switching on his transmitter, setting the frequency. He would be going to listen. Two dozen men in the base mess would be wondering how he was getting on. No, Forbush thought, they had probably forgotten him already. Weeks, or even months, later somebody might say "I wonder how Dick's getting on up at Royds?" Weeks after that he might wonder again and bother to ask Alex if Dick was still up at Royds.

Forbush switched on his radio, carefully set the transmission frequency and waited for the set to warm up as he drew the heavily padded earphones on.

"Hullo Scott Base, Hullo Scott Base, this is ZLYR Cape Royds calling ZLQ Scott Base, how do you read me? Over." Forbush spoke very distinctly, a little clipped and nervous he thought, and he had again the strange feeling that he was being overheard. He began to repeat the call as Alex's voice crackled loudly through the receiver.

"Hullo ZLYR. Hullo ZLYR. This is ZLQ Scott Base. I'm

reading you merit three Dick, merit three, how do you read me? Over."

"Loud and clear Alex, loud and clear. I've got nothing to report up here. Good day today. No penguins yet. I don't know how far out the ice edge is still. Have you got any report on the break-out? Have you any report on ice conditions? Over." Forbush found he was shaking slightly and faintly embarrassed at having to make what seemed a trivial enquiry for the sake of having something to say.

'Glad you're settling in all right Dick, glad you're settling in. I have no accurate report on ice conditions, no accurate report but there was a flight in from Christchurch this afternoon and they said the ice appeared to be fast well north of Beaufort Island, well north of Beaufort. That's all I can tell you Dick. That's all. I have no other message for you. Over."

Beaufort Island. Well past Beaufort Island—that would make the ice edge sixty, seventy, eighty miles north, Forbush thought in sudden confusion. He didn't know what to say and then, with a flood of warmth in the pit of his stomach remembered his telegram.

"Hullo ZLQ. Hullo Alex. That's a bit of a shock about the ice Alex. I suppose the poor little beggars will be a day or two late. Alex would you take a telegram for me? Would you take a telegram? It's to Miss Barbara Reilly 115 Grosvenor Street Christchurch." He paused while the address was repeated scratchily over the receiver like the name of some utterly foreign person in a remote country.

"Here's the message quote safe at Royds but no company stop wish you were here signed Forbush unquote. She knows I'm not emotional." He felt apologetic, wildly emotional, and discovered he was gripping the microphone strongly and stickily.

The silence descended on him again like cool water closing over his head, as if he had reached up into the colourful, bright and noisy world and then sunk back into a pool of quiet.

He cooked a dehydrated meat-bar stew in his pressure cooker scorning the frozen fresh meats in his store and even forgetting his beer, and then climbed into bed to read, no longer aware of the hut and its relics but secure and contained by his possessions. At midnight, when the light outside was soft and grey with dusk he turned off the heaters, poked his tongue out at the yellow rabbit, and slept.

CHAPTER THREE

On Friday, 21 October, at 3 p.m. Forbush saw a skua gull fly overhead. Snow was falling in light puffy balls like mimosa blossom. There was no wind and the day seemed warm. He was standing in the middle of Pony Lake alone in the silence. Through the fog he could barely see the Cape rocks and the hut so that it appeared to him that his was the last corner of a world overtaken by a cold white destruction, and that only his own will preserved the frozen pond on which he stood and the land under the pond like a substantial cloud on which he fled endlessly through dismal heavens. The snow fell thickly, clotting on his shoulders and arms, on his feet and in the fur edge of his anarak hood. It clung to the blue ice in small clumps as if each crystal was drawn to another by the infinitely small and slow convulsions of its ordered molecules. From the ice itself hoar flowers grew, their delicate ribbed sprays and petals wavering slightly with every subdued movement of the air. Forbush thought that if he stood long enough he might be able to see the petals grow, layer by layer of their fragile hexagonal structure, as they drew increase from the strangely humid air.

What made him look up and towards the dim outline of the Cape? He saw the skua's shape flicker above the rocks for an instant and did not believe. He saw it again moments later flying in from the sea across the rookery and towards him, then ranging north over the hillside colony sites, then south again in a low circular glide. He stood quite still and breathless, feeling the pounding of his heart. The skua swooped low over a large rock, tail fanned and down, its feet splayed and outstretched for landing, its wing beats rapid and braking its flight, then in one smooth movement changing to a slower rhythmic forward thrust as it drew back its legs and launched into a banking turn towards Forbush, who still stood silent.

The skua came in low over the lake towards him through

the falling snow, direct, functional and menacing until he could see its black eyes above the heavy hooked beak, the speckled grey and brown of its breast feathers and the firm sculptured lines of its white-edged wings. Casually and disdainfully it dropped a wing-tip, banked away and then, as if it flowed on a smooth current of air, turned and swung up behind and over Forbush's head, southwards.

"Hey!" shouted Forbush, but could the sound have travelled further than his own lips and the echoing passages between throat and eardrums?

The skua soared hawk-like and vanished in the mist towards Cape Barne. Forbush walked down to Access Beach and searched for penguin tracks in the fresh snow. It was unmarked.

Bored and a little depressed he cooked himself a celebratory dinner of kidneys, bacon and steak that evening after he had kept a pointless radio schedule with Scott Base. He thought he could hear through the radio's crackle laughter and talk, the tap-tap-squelch of cans of beer being opened in the base radio room. By midnight he finished his fourth detective novel. Snow was still falling, gathering in the corners of the window panes as he went to sleep.

On Saturday by ten o'clock in the morning a twenty-knot wind was blowing and the air outside was thick with drift snow. The wind made a malign whimper round the hut so he stayed in bed until the late afternoon. By then most of Friday's fresh and powdering snow, easily lifted by the wind, had blown away and all that remained of the mild blizzard was billowing clouds of drift across the lower slopes of Mount Erebus and the ice falls south beyond Cape Evans. The snowdrift at the hut door was level with the top step and Forbush sank through it above his knees when he floundered outside to let the wind blow the stuffy warmth of his corner of the hut out of his eyes. It was like stepping into a chill bubblebath.

Wise enough not to eat during a day of lying up, Forbush began to cook himself a dinner of curried steak. In his search for spices he broke open a packet of U.S. Navy survival rations left in the hut by some past travellers. Inside was a pamphlet setting down in minute detail how the ration pack should be used and giving daily menus for survival periods ranging from one week to thirty days. In large lettering at the end of the pamphlet was written "Do Not Panic. Remember. Help Is Near." Forbush found some excellent chilli powder and some inferior lemon drink crystals.

He took a can of beer from a case carefully stowed above the stoves so that its contents would not freeze. The hut was warm, full of domestic clutter and good cooking smells. He drank another can of beer and cleaned his filthy fingernails while he waited for his curry to cook and for his dehydrated mashed potato powder to swell and cook to a satisfying fluffiness.

He drank another can of beer with his curry and then ate a can of strawberries. He put the three empty beer cans on the floor and jumped on them until they were squashed flat. His duties and responsibilities as custodian of a monument weighed heavily on him. Must not make a mess. Must be tidy. Must bury the rubbish. Must avoid fire. Must not spill paraffin on the floor. Must not squirt beer on hallowed relics. Damn it, why haven't I got a uniform?

Forbush went out scowling to fill his box with snow and staggered through the fresh drifts feeling all gleaming and radiant in the orange of the late sunlight. He didn't even bother to look for the penguins. It's Saturday night and everybody is having a party but me. Barbara would be having a party. Starshot would be having a party. Alex Fisher would be having a party. Everyone at Scott Base would be singing and jumping about and already a little drunk. The rum jar would be on the table and the radiogram would be turned up noisy and high and John King would be tuning his guitar in the corner with a wild look in his eye and Hank the Medical Corps man from the airstrip would be tuning his little mahogany-coloured ukulele and thinking of a bawdy song which nobody had heard before and there would be radio-telephone calls to home, faint, fading and returning voices of loved ones trying not to sound emotional over 2200 miles of eccentric radio circuit.

In Christchurch the new willow leaves would be leaning over the River Avon and the weeping elms and pine trees and chestnuts would scent the velvet spring air in the misty dark beside the river. The ducks would be calm and fulfilled with the spring, quiet and going about their courtships as carelessly as ever and the young trout would be jumping in quiet backwaters where insects dropped plumply into their open mouths. The cold wind seized Forbush and gripped his chest, its fingers rippling round his back and under his shirt. He dug furiously with his small shovel at the snow bank and ran back to the hut clutching his box of snow close so that the crystals danced and shook down his neck and settled in a freezing band around his stomach.

He washed his dishes and swept the floor, took out his clarinet, three cans of beer, a writing pad and his pen.

"Barbara—I don't know what I'm doing here and I don't know what you're doing. Not grieving for me, surely, not missing me? Please insert the following advertisement in the Christchurch *Press*. 'Wanted for Isolated Seaside Resort. Capable woman to act as custodian of historic monument. Uniforms provided. Duties also to include care and maintenance of one penguin biologist (youthful). Apply with references and recent photograph to R. J. Forbush, Cape Royds, the Riviera of the South.'

"The penguins are late. There is absolutely nobody here. I am the only person in the whole world. In fact I am the whole world because the rest of it blew away in a blizzard last week. There is absolutely no point, under these circumstances, in my writing to you at all but I live in the hope that, by some miraculous contortion of the universe, you will have been preserved alive and still loving sufficient for this letter to seek you out. Antarctica diminishes me. It gives nothing back. Each day I deliver up to it a little more of myself. The other day the sun attempted the theft of my eyes. Then the ice attempted to transmogrify my good and honest organic nature to conform to the simple and practical laws by which it continues its philistinic existence. I resisted of course.

"But Barbara, the horrible thought occurs (you will understand I am getting a little drunk) that the ice might be entirely right. It's sheer presumption to suppose that the organic orientation of matter is any more likely than the inorganic, it's sheer human vanity to imagine the soul is any more immutable than a piece of rock, a pebble in a penguin's nest. Draw for me, the ice said, the line between life and not-life. Then the skua gull zoomed at me out of the fog (it was snowing at the time). The thing was so self-contained. It just flew around on its own business and there seemed to be quite as much to its flying as to my walking, in fact, as an acrobatic performer, the bird was much more clever than I. I called to it but it didn't answer.

"Barbara. I'm obsessed with the urgency of returning to you before the ice diminishes me into an icicle (ick!).

"Barbara. You were very soft and good, so very warm and soft mouthed the night before I left. I am afraid that when I come home I'll be so hard that I hurt you.

"Perhaps I'll soften again when the birds come, when the sea comes, when there's water to hear on the gravelly beach. My heart's frozen in by all this ice. To write 'I love you' seems as pointless as trying to unfreeze the sea by breathing on it.

"God—there's so much to do here and it won't get started. I've really stopped believing in penguins. They're such damned improbable creatures in any case. Day after day goes by and they don't come. They don't come. There's no sign. No telling."

Forbush stopped writing and finished the fourth can of beer. He put his head on his hands and looked out of the window at the long black shadows and the golden rocks above them. The night was surely warm. Surely it was calm and peaceful, a night to wander in, to be caressed by radiance, to glow, to be part of the sun. He got up quickly and almost ran outside. There was no wind now and the Cape glowed black and gold with utter starkness and clarity. The mountain was capped by a billowing plume of smoke cloud that seemed to tower up, to lean out over Forbush and the small grey hut like the towering hand of God quivering with its throbbing smoky veins and all the strength of its wind-taut sinews. The cold beat him back so that he stepped slowly backwards towards the door, arms outstretched downwards, fingers splayed stiff until they touched the rough, cold wood. He climbed the steps slowly, not to appear defeated, and closed the doors. Without reading the letter he scrawled his signature, sealed the envelope and addressed it, then sat with his head in his hands and his eyes tightly closed.

Slowly warmth returned and he opened his eyes to blink in the light. The table, the hut, everything looked exactly the same. "Well that was a bit bloody melodramatic," he said aloud. He shook his head until his eyes ached heavily.

Forbush decided to have a wash. He took down two more cans of beer and went to inspect the large iron pot which stood on Shackleton's stove. It was fairly rusty but not too bad. "I'll probably be accused of desecration, grave robbing, necromancy, nepotism and obscene exposure for this," he said and began to giggle. He pumped up the Primus until its pressure was explosive, filled the pot with snow and set it to heat. The ancient blue and white enamel pitcher caught his eye so he set it on the table beside his soap, toothbrush, toothpaste and face-cloth.

Two cans of beer later Forbush sat cross-legged on the table playing Ravel's *Bolero* on his clarinet and squinting at the pot-bellied water pitcher. The pot was half-full of lukewarm rusty water so he filled it with snow again and reached for more beer. The case fell off the shelf on to the floor so that when he opened a fresh can it squirted gaily in his eyes, and ears, over his face and dripped still foaming off his beard on to his knees. Solemn and spluttering Forbush put a forefinger over the hole in the can, shook it and squirted the rabbit which dripped and continued to grin.

When he played *Jesu Joy of Man's Desiring* on his clarinet Forbush almost cried, but noticed in time that his bath water was hot. Feeling rather sober he stood up and undressed. Freedom. He stood over one of the heaters and felt the warm air rising up his legs, buttocks, back, and tingling on the back of his neck. The hair on his legs and thighs seemed to ripple with the warmth of the current like fog grass on a windy hill. He clasped his arms around his chest feeling the greasiness of his warm skin, then bent his head down and to his left shoulder, first scratching it with his beard, reflective and then licking the salt sweat. It was a good taste, a good animal taste which made him feel that he possessed himself again.

Carefully and shaking a little, almost shivering, he washed his whole body. Then with a slightly desperate sense of defiance he filled the pitcher with water, walked steadily outside to stand in the snow and pour it over his head. For a moment his body was relaxed, his skin warm and silky, then quite quickly it grew taut and stretched with the frost. He ran inside with the pitcher and dressed.

On Sunday, 23 October, Forbush slept late. In the afternoon he walked east over the ribbed volcanic ridges into Backdoor Bay and then up from its inner shores to Blue Lake. On a little moraine island in the middle of the lake he found some orange lichens clinging in the rock crevices like tiny clusters of limpets on a tidal shore. At four o'clock as he climbed the scoria slopes at the seaward end of the lake he saw three snow petrels flying very high like delicate leaves blown far up into the sky's greatest depth of blue, released and joyous in their quick soaring. He thought of the white birds which the Maoris say come to guide the spirits of the dead to Te Reinga o Te Wairua, the resting place of departed souls.

On Monday afternoon, as he sat scanning seaward again from his favourite shelter among the rocks of the Cape he thought he could see, miles out over the ice, the black hump of the seal sleeping beside a crack in the floes.

He began in these days to find a certain peace in the silence and no longer talked aloud to himself. He felt clear-eyed and unstrained, accepting, and no longer anxious for the penguins. In fact, he hardly believed they would come at all and was content to live simply, day by day, trusting in the mountain, the sun which now no longer dipped below the western ranges at midnight but lit the ice and the black hillsides with pale golden fire.

He began to read *The Torrents of Spring* saddened at Turgenev's understanding, rueful for love, yet untroubled. Shut off from the realities of wordly life he could enjoy his own idealism in a comfortable certainty. He became sure that human beings were pure and good and that life in the world would be rich and gentle when he returned, full of slow and painless growth towards truth, knowledge, good uncluttered science. Like Sanin before his disillusionment "It was as though a curtain, a light, thin curtain, hung faintly swaying before his inner eye; and behind that curtain he felt—he felt the presence of a young, motionless divine face with a tender smile on her lips and stern, feignedly stern, lowered eyelids. And this face was not the face of Gemma but the face of happiness itself!"

On the warm evening of Tuesday, 25 October, after failing to make radio contact with base Forbush sat high on the Cape rocks. He had found a small nook like a throne from which a pagan god might have directed the spiritual travail of his subjects. A flat wind-smoothed boulder fitted his back when he squatted down with hunched knees, and rocks on either side kept the air still. The ground beneath his feet was covered with small round scoria pebbles, pitted like pumice stones, like the calcified skeletons of ambulant sea creatures. From this golden throne he could look north, seawards, but the far shore of the Sound was shut off from his view and the mountain, although he remained aware of it, smoked behind his sight. His vision seemed to be directed seawards as if all his power of sight were concentrated into one narrow searching beam which scanned the northerly ice probing deep into the blue caves and hollows of the icebergs themselves. The night being warm, because it was quite windless, Forbush had brought his clarinet to the Cape and now played it carefully and precisely with slightly stiff lips and fingers. The notes were contained within the confines of his throne as if they had individual substance and gathered, as he blew them, to dance above his head like soap bubbles. He felt his heart being overwhelmed with relief because there was no wind to carry them away.

At ten o'clock he played the flute part from the slow movement of the fifth Brandenburg Concerto, a sombre and delicate air to fit the rhythm of the slowly rolling sun. All the shadows on the ice seemed to point towards him, the long, rectangular darkness of the iceberg stranded off Cape Bird, the menacing spearhead of shade cast by a curious and conical pressure hummock off Access Beach. He longed for a tree, even the remnant of a tree, a dead trunk with stark and silver arms raised to the sun, shining among the salty summer grass of a coastal hillside.

For a time he warmed his fingers by drawing on his mitts and holding his fists tight under his arms. Then he played the adagio movement from Beethoven's A Minor Quartet, marked *A Restored One's Holy Song of Thanksgiving to God*, a rapturous sound.

Throughout this playing he watched the penguin which was so distant and so small that it was no more significant than the speck of dust one can sometimes see floating on the surface of the eye when looking into the empty light of the summer sky. The first penguin was merely like the speck of beginning life in the yolk of a new-laid egg, its movements equally slight and equally irresistible because it was driven, dancing and rolling, shimmering and vibrant down the horizon of the ice with all the will to live of a whole world behind it. To Forbush it appeared that the penguin was being drawn by his music and guided by the searching shaft of his sight.

In the eye of his mind he could see the penguin stumbling and sliding over the ice surface. Its feet, scaly and nerveless, with animal claws, made an almost inaudible scratching on the bare ice like seeds rattling in the dry seed pods of a broom thicket stirring in the soft wind of a hot autumn day. Plump and bright-eyed, the penguin walked quickly southwards still clean and shining from the sea, its white breast feathers bearing the golden sheen of the sun. It walked with its flippers outstretched to balance each forward thrust of its short thick thighs, its head nodding from side to side, always attentive to its course, turned sometimes back over sloping shoulders, sometimes skywards, careful against enemies, curious for companions. When it reached a crack in the ice it stopped, standing very erect, then leaning forward and peering down, its flippers stretched back as if to divine the depths and limits of the obstacle with its short thick beak. Then it jumped with stiff legs, fell forward on its smooth breast and tobogganned, thrusting forward with paddling legs and flippers until it reached rough ice again or a soft snow dune, tail erect, head up and searching ahead, like a plump black and white gondola.

Forbush ceased his playing and put down his clarinet. It seemed to him that the Cape was no longer silent and that the sunlit night itself had a sound and movement, that the rocks were living and that the ice was no longer an enemy but a kindly element of life. He stood up and rubbed the cold of the rocks out of his buttocks, slapping his windproof trousers noisily. It would be after midnight by the time the penguin arrived at the beach. He took a cake of chocolate from his anarak pocket and ate it, feeling the warmth of its sweetness spread out from his stomach almost immediately.

Now the penguin had definition, he could see the outstretched flippers and the bob of each step it took. There was a certain hesitance about its progress as if it was not sure whether its destination lay close at hand or if its journey must extend into a lifetime of precarious footsteps. Half a mile from the coast it stopped and appeared to go to sleep, head slumped into its hunched shoulders, flippers held close to its breast.

Forbush felt angry for a moment, then amused.

"What a stupid bird – you've taken all this time coming to see me and now you stop out there and go to sleep. Come on. Come on. You're late you fool and you've got work to do."

Through his binoculars the penguin looked familiar and absurd yet not without dignity as it rocked back on its heels to lift its cold toes off the ice. Forbush wondered if the penguin knew it was first and that there was no real hurry. Perhaps it seemed that the rookery would be just as lonely as its long journey over the ice.

"I wonder how far you've come. The ice must be incredibly heavy. You'll certainly have a long wait for your next meal my little penguin. Come on. Come on. Stop sleeping there." He felt a sudden glow of excitement and stamped impatiently on the stones.

"Come on."

His sense of being alone had already receded as if he had stepped out into bright air from a long dim-lit tunnel. Memories of the past week stirred in his mind and it seemed as if they had happened to another person, as if he, Forbush, had slept and dreamed unhappily. Life was suddenly urgent again.

"Come on. Come on."

He heard the sound of his feet on the pebbles, new and sharp, as if he had become detached from them and was no longer a still and timeless part of the frozen ground, the frozen past, as if his skin and flesh had become firm and distinct with boundaries. He shivered, flexed his shoulders, stretched his back muscles and stood on one leg.

"Come on penguin, you stupid penguin." This time he shouted it, his mittened hands cupped to his mouth, his head flung back. The penguin did not stir.

Half an hour later, just after midnight, while Forbush was squatting hunched against his rock again, almost dozing and now cold and stiff, intensely aware of his shivering, aching limbs, the penguin raised its head, made a darting glance first to one side and then to the other though still with hunched shoulders, then stretched its neck, ruffled its thick black shoulder feathers until it looked like an anxious hedgehog, flapped its flippers and began to walk, at first quite slowly with deliberate and pompous steps, then rapidly swinging each hip stiffly forward like a plump old lady, craning its head and peering from side to side quite grotesquely.

"Ah," said Forbush. "Now don't stop, for God's sake don't stop."

He stood up and with his clarinet tucked under his arm walked slowly down from the Cape. The penguin kept coming, faster now as if it suddenly knew where it was going and had remembered its purpose. In front of the ice hummock it stopped to peer to each side, weighing the relative advantages of each way round. It took the shoreside route but came to a deep crack before which it stopped to bow and peer, hunch its shoulders, ruffle its feathers, edge sideways until, almost on the verge of stopping for another sleep, it cleared the gap with a sudden stiff jump and came on running until it reached the stranded growler. This, it decided, was an obstacle which must be conquered. It would go over the top, an act more easily proposed than executed as it discovered during several pig-headed and scrambling attempts to mount the sheerest face. Eventually it hopped, jumped, scraped and strutted its way to the top and bravely launched itself breast forward down the shoreward face to land upside down at the bottom. After kicking its legs and waving its flippers as if it believed these to be wings the penguin marched resolutely for the shore.

Here Forbush now stood feeling slightly embarrassed as if some ceremony of considerable import was about to take place. He wondered if he should play his clarinet in greeting, and blew a high sweet note. The penguin stopped, legs wide apart and flippers outstretched. It lifted its beak into the air and rapidly swung its head from side to side.

"Damn it, the thing's conducting me," Forbush said.

The penguin walked forward again, jumped the tide-crack with abandon, not even bothering to consider its depth, and mounted the beach ice until it stood in the soft drift snow. Forbush stood quite still because he was not at all sure what to do. It seemed this meeting had some significance and that he, in all his human glory, six feet high and one hundred and sixty pounds, should in some way honour this valiant eighteen-inch, fourteen-pound wanderer who had come so clean and glorious over seventy or eighty miles of frozen sea. The penguin went to sleep.

"To hell with you then—and damn you for being unsociable," Forbush said, lighthearted at last. He turned and walked up the bank to the rookery to stop again when he saw the penguin was following. It came quite slowly as if to emphasise its indifference to Forbush, but steadily up the bank and then across the rookery making for the southern slopes with an air of self-contained detachment. Halfway through the hill colonies it stopped and said *Aaark*, repeating the call twice with outstretched flippers. It seemed lost and therefore went to sleep while Forbush stood some distance away, patient now and watchful.

After five minutes the penguin woke, walked rapidly twenty yards to its left without one indecisive movement and stopped on a nest mound beside a large boulder and facing the hut. Here it stood for a moment before taking two steps forward to bend its head down, pick up a small pebble in its beak, turn slowly round, take two steps on to the next mound and place the stones, very gently and with a very precise movement of its craned head, its flippers stretched back for balance. Forbush could clearly see the white rings around its round and dark brown eyes.

In the absence of immediate competition the penguin appeared satisfied that its claim to the nest was valid and prepared to make its ecstatic display. Standing very erect it slowly raised its beak straight up to the sky until its neck was stretched like the neck of a diving gannet and its flippers were outstretched and pointing downwards as if it tried to turn itself into an arrowhead, a spear, a rocket missile directed at the heavens, a potent and masculine shape which would direct its cry, the woeful and pagan music of its sex in the soft blue depths of the sky.

Forbush stood stiff and still, attentive for the sound of life beginning, feeling that his heart was parched, frozen, waiting to be released, that his heart was swelling, rising into his throat, throbbing and pumping as the first soft, harsh beats of the penguin's call beat far down in its shining breast, then in its throat, so that he saw the rhythmic, rising spasm of its tightened throat muscles even before he heard the drumming. The slow beat began like the threshing of flails on a threshing floor falling rhythmically on rich and heavy ears of ripened grain and then quickening, rising in the bird's convulsing throat like the sudden convulsion of stormwind among forest trees until the sound burst from its opened beak. *Ka. Ka. Ka. Kakakakaaa, kakakakaaa, kakakakaaa.* The penguin's flippers beat slowly and stiffly in time with its music.

The sun bright in his eyes Forbush felt slow warmth and exhaustion creep over him as the penguin ceased its singing, its wavering neck relaxed and its head settled on its shoulders hunched for sleep.

Silence. The world was peopled with avian spirits which soared around Forbush and brushed his face so that it stung no longer with the midnight frost. At peace he walked away, across the frozen lake to his cold and silent hut.

CHAPTER FOUR

"EVERY day begins," thought Forbush, "as if a curtain was being raised upon some immense and magic and splendid inactivity of the indifferent universe, as if the day's whole purpose was to prove that nothing is different, nothing has changed. This is a huge joke. We are fooled into believing, because life begins and life ends, because there is being born and being dead, that these acts are marks in time, a careful prescription of existence. In fact, and quite paradoxically it seems, such events change nothing—but I am alive!" This he shouted and sat up in bed. Penguins! He rushed outside in his underwear.

A strong wind blew up the Sound and the drift snow was hard and gritty. The cold chilled him instantly to the depths of his stomach and bit his fingers. Three penguins sat widely spaced on the sheltered southern slopes of the rookery. The world was hugely alive and roaring with the wind.

Forbush dressed quickly while the Primus hissed to boil water for his breakfast porridge. He talked to the rabbit. "Ha ha! Alphonse, you silly grinning rabbit, you didn't think the penguins were coming did you, you didn't believe in them, you just sat there and grinned stupidly didn't you Alphonse, but you were wrong. They've come, Alphonse, they've come." He threw a dirty sock at Alphonse and almost dislodged him from his curtain wire.

By the end of the week there were almost a hundred birds dotted round the rookery and the first skua gulls had flown over, circled, inspected, stayed a while and moved on south or hesitantly back to the north. Forbush had little to do except take daily population counts and observe for long hours at a time the penguins' behaviour. The Cape was still his favourite observatory position for he could see both the new arrivals straggling in over the ice and the nest-building residents.

On Saturday morning at ten o'clock a helicopter flew high

over the Cape, a fluorescent red bird whose soaring seemed to be aimed towards the smoking summit of Erebus. It was like a lark hovering above spring pastures so high that all you knew of it was its rippling song. Forbush gazed upwards, eyes burned by the cold blue light, and then looked anxiously at the penguins. The helicopter appeared to be hovering indecisively but then he saw it begin the slow, wide spiral of descent, lowering itself with delicate and entirely functional precision towards Pony Lake.

When it had fallen to a thousand feet above the lake Forbush stood up. The standing penguins raised their heads glancing up and around, quick and nervous. The sitting birds, squatting like black and white bottles atilt their half-built nests, spread their flippers wide slowly, peering upwards, wary, with outstretched necks. Forbush clenched his fists as the helicopter began the next gentle loop of its spiral, six hundred, five hundred, four hundred feet. The first penguin broke, began to run or scuttle, neck outstretched, beak open, flippers spread wide aback like fearful fingers, head feathers erect and angular. It jumped around boulders in its path and fell forward on top of a sitting bird sheltering in the stony lee. They fought. Forbush imagined he could hear, under the thunderous thudding of the helicopter's rotor blades, the thump and drum of their frenzied beating flippers and the snapping of their beaks. Beating and tearing at each other the birds rolled down a pebbly slope, parted and rushed bleeding towards the shore, now part of a frantic crowd of birds all running, jumping, sliding, scrambling towards the sea ice, northwards into the sun and at last obscured from Forbush by a rolling cloud of snow that boiled from under the gale of the helicopter's rotor blades as it settled slowly and jerkily on to the lake ice.

Forbush stood still, feeling this monstrous and mechanical wind ripping at his eyes and nostrils, cutting at his face with vicious particles of snow and grit. As the engine died the boiling snow cloud rippled out from its landing point to leave the helicopter settled like a stick flung violently into calm water surrounded by the widening waves of its impact. The rotor blades swung powerfully still but slowing, dying. Forbush stood in the empty rookery as the crewman and two pilots emerged to stand silent, legs apart, like figures on a grotesque primitive painting, in front of their aircraft looking at him. He said nothing but faced them across fifty yards of chill air until it seemed that minutes were passing and the rotor blades at last swung to a stop.

"Hey!" said one of the pilots.

"The fools, the bloody fools, I don't suppose they even know there's a rookery here," Forbush said to himself. He rasied a hand in greeting and began to walk down the hill. The three men walked stiffly to meet him.

"Say, we thought we'd find some penguins here. We brought some mail for you too. Where they all gone, those penguins? Gee we were real sure we'd see some of them here."

"Gentlemen," said Forbush as he stopped at the lake edge. "Much as I am delighted to receive you I must regretfully tell you that the penguins declined the pleasure of your company. In fact you scared the living daylights out of the poor, stupid animals *and they all ran bleeding into the sea!*"

Silence. The pilot, the co-pilot and the crewman all stared at Forbush and then, briefly, at each other. Still holding his hat in one dirty fist (he had torn it from his head in the last gust of wind from the landing helicopter), hair stiffly awry, with grizzled beard and swollen, snowburned nose Forbush glared back in an attitude of rigid indignation. "*You bloody idiots!*"

"Well, gee, I'm sorry." The pilot took a step forward beginning to extend a hand, stiff in his bright orange flying suit, nodding with the bulk of his helmet. "Anyway we brought you some mail."

Forbush sat down on a nearby stone and rested his chin in his hands for a moment. Then he gestured slowly for them to come to him and they walked with mincing and careful steps across the slick ice to the shore.

"You're new here, I suppose," said Forbush.

"Yeah, well, gee, I just got in here yesterday. We're just having a look around. It's a fine place and well gee would you like a cigarette? Have you got a cigarette Johnny?" The co-pilot solemnly unzipped one of his many zippers (his arms, legs, chest and buttocks seemed to be covered with them as if, by some curious requirement of his profession, he was equipped with a multiplicity of retractable limbs to be carefully zippered up when not in use) and produced cigarettes which he handed to the pilot.

"Here, have a smoke. Are you feelin' all right? Well you see we just got in here yesterday and we heard about these penguins so we thought we'd just take a look around. Will you have a smoke? Anyway somebody said one of you Kiwi boys was up here so we asked if we could drag anything up for you and they gave us this mail bag. Anyway my name's Al Weiser glad to meet you will you have a smoke?"

Forbush had appeared to hear little of this speech and still sat fingering his beard with the three orange figures grouped round him looking down with concern.

"Thank you no. I prefer these special dehydrated New Zealand cigarettes," Forbush said eventually. "Sit down Mr. Weiser, gentlemen. Gentlemen these penguins which you have come to see have all run away because your helicopter frightened them. In a few hours they will, I hope, recover and return to their nests. They have, however, had a long and difficult journey to reach this rookery because the open sea is about seventy-five miles away instead of two miles away. Imagine, gentlemen, walking seventy-five miles on legs three inches long. Imagine starving for forty days while you build a nest out of stones, court a wife, fight off the competition, copulate, attend your wife in her confinement and incubate her eggs and then, before you can end your fast, walking seventy-five miles on your three-inch legs to find the sea. Imagine that, while you are beginning this long and hazardous endeavour—and you're doing it not from choice but from incontrovertible instinct—a great noisy red monster descends on you from out of the sky in a gale of wind and a cloud of snow and three little orange men get out of it. Gentlemen, you run. You fall over the cliff and break your neck, you get hysterical and trample on your neighbour who batters you until you are bleeding with wounds from his nasty little flippers. You run because you don't know you've got a good chance of dying anyway because the ice and your instinct will kill you. You just run away from that big red bird and those three little orange men. Gentlemen, please give me my bag of mail and go away quickly and tell your friends about the little penguins."

Forbush stood up, a wild and strangely patriarchal figure before which the orange men slowly backed away. The crewman scuttled over the ice to fetch the mail bag.

"Yes sir, yes sir," said the pilot. "Yes sir, we'll certainly tell them. We're real sorry, Mr. Forbush, we're real sorry. We just saw that little helo pad up on the hill there but we thought it was a long way to walk so we thought we'd land right here on the lake. But we didn't know we were going to hurt the penguins Mr. Forbush. I mean well we'll tell them, well here's your mail and I guess we'd better get moving along or our engine'll freeze up on us so then what'd the penguins do? Well I guess we'll be seeing you again some time. Have a good time up here. Gee you Kiwis do some wild things. You bet. So long."

Forbush sat on his rock clutching the mail bag while the starter motors wheezed, the engine coughed and raced and the rotors whirled. He disappeared in a cloud of snow which did not settle until the helicopter was out of sight beyond Flagstaff Hill.

"Forbush the magician," he thought as the snow cloud whirled round him. "Summoning up red monsters and little orange men and banishing them at will. Damn. Damn. Damn. I felt like company."

Swinging his mail bag (there's not much in it—a parcel of some sort—aaah! Cake!) he wandered over the abandoned rookery until he could look out over the sea ice. The still scuttling figures were widespread as if they had been scattered across the ice like tiny black seeds from a gigantic hand, north, south and west. As he watched several of the nearer birds stopped, shuffled nervously looking back at the rookery and went to sleep. He knew they would stay like that for hours.

"I had better attend my duties as sole Postmaster and Potentate of Cape Royds." He remembered, slightly aggrieved, that he had not had time to give his own letters to the pilot for posting at Scott Base.

Obviously the best place to read one's mail was in bed.

Although the outside temperature had risen since his arrival until now at midday it was only about twenty degrees of frost—warm if there was no wind—the hut still took hours of heating each day. He sat in his sleeping bag, carefully cutting the lead-sealed string on the mail bag and shook the letters on to his splayed knees.

Yes. Cake, it was surely cake securely parcelled in a round tin and addressed in his mother's careful, round writing. Also a letter from his mother; a postcard offering him cut rate use of a honeymoon cottage at a North Island beach resort, a circular advising him to join the Public Service Investment Society, a bank statement reflecting excessive living before departure to the frozen south, a notice demanding payment of dues to the New Zealand Workers' Union which he had received regularly each quarter for three years since his last University vacation job, a Christchurch Public Library notice about overdue books, a Christmas card from his Member of Parliament (a miserable excuse for self-advertisement), and a letter addressed "Forbush the Great, Cape Royds, Antarctica." The Post Office had performed one of its daily minor miracles of delivery.

His mother wrote that the lettuces were growing very rapidly, it appeared that the tomato season might be good, there had never been so much asparagus about in living memory, she had seen his arrival at McMurdo Sound in an American aeroplane on TV and why did all the men who wintered over look so morose? She hoped he was not lonely and that he washed his socks. Hard work was the best cure for depression. "'The Lord is My Shepherd, I shall not want, He maketh me to lie down in Green Pastures . . .' Richard dear, we are so looking forward to you coming home and hate to think of you alone in that bitter place."

The sun shone in the north windows so that the strong, dark grain of the teak table took on a glistening sheen. It's almost hot, thought Forbush and leaned over to light the Primus so that his face was washed in sunlight that seemed to reach and cleanse every pore of his skin.

"Dear Forbush—Your letter found me so I have faith enough to give you your due in addressing this in return."

He had kept Barbara's letter to read last. Like the elegance of her writing, her style was dignified and remote yet her mood enquiring.

"But I haven't posted it," he suddenly realised. "What the hell is she talking about . . . oh." He remembered posting her a note the day after his arrival at Scott Base and sank back in his bed holding her letter in both hands across his chest, immersed again in the peculiar convulsion of time and space which now seemed to be a condition of his existence so that he felt curiously immortal.

"And how is Our Lady Mother of the Snows, Antarctica? What is it like, Forbush, to tug life from her cold breast? Have the eternal beasts come south to join you? Are you one with them, a struggling animal, or are you still big and proud?

"I sit here in the close spring sunshine surrounded by all these books. The breath of you from the south turns this library into a fossil forest of knowledge. Before you went away it lived. Now I can hear the sombre rumble of the lawn mower cutting back the cautious growth of academic grass and can smell the spring smell of new mowing, green as life. If I walk to my window and look down from under these eaves I can see sparrows bathing in the dust. The students wander, aimless as summer bees. I'm so sick, so heart sick of universities. I want you, all strength and action. Forbush, I'll have to wait, you fool, why must you leave me behind?

"Thank you for your telegram. When you come home I will say 'I love you.' " Signed "B".

She says so little, thought Forbush. And yet there is nothing more to say. Come on penguins, come on, get it over with, breed, mate, copulate, lay, incubate, rear, die or live, swim away, swim north and let me go. Come on, come on, release me.

The pot of water on the Primus boiled over. Forbush unfolded a slip of paper in Barbara's envelope, a clipping from the *Waimate Daily Advertiser*. "Crusader on a Bicycle Visits Waimate—A spiritual revival is the answer to the mental illness of the nation in the opinion of much-travelled visitor to Waimate 51-year-old Mr. Arnold G. Brooker, of Wellington. Mr. Brooker has travelled more than 50,000 miles by bicycle during a four-year crusade to prove that in the spiritual realms lies the answer to mental illness. He has distributed more than 32,000 leaflets on psychiatric reform . . . 'Psychology and psychiatry are the sciences which will enable us to understand the healing power which individuals could have to chase evil spirits out of people,' Mr. Brooker said."

"Just to show we are all still crazy," Barbara had scrawled on the bottom. "Why not come home and enjoy it in comfort?"

"O the curious world," Forbush thought. "Why is it so easy not to feel part of it? Why is it so good, so bitter and real to be alone?" He skewered the cutting on a nail stuck in the ration box wall above his head.

As the days passed and he stomped on his regular rounds through the rookery Forbush felt himself becoming more and more possessive of the Cape, the ice, the mountain and the sky. Only the sun seemed without his reach and yet he lived with it in a state of easy trust, almost conspiracy. He and the sun were joint protectors of the penguins, regulators of their lives, omnipotent watchers over their instinctive progress towards summer fruitfulness, the vulnerable moment of birth. By the first week of November there were a thousand birds on the rookery slopes and others were still coming, in groups of a dozen or twenty, or sometimes alone, or in twos and threes.

His first act each day was to walk down to the beach to welcome the morning travellers coming briskly off the ice, clean and shining in the sun. Then he started his counting rounds, first with the highest colony on the northern slope. By now the separate colony areas into which the rookery was divided were distinct—fifteen of them ranging in population from half a dozen pairs to more than a hundred. To count the number of pairs and nests in each colony took a careful hour or more for he found that he had to visit each one in turn because the larger colonies were too widely spread to be scanned accurately with binoculars. The birds took little notice of him and yet were not sufficiently strongly established on their nests to defend them when he stood too close. When he walked through a colony they backed nervously away, sometimes running a yard or two then turning to hiss at him like husky snakes, flippers stretched back and heads, with white-ringed eyes wide and staring, thrust forward.

The days were full of their sound, the drumming and trumpeting of the ecstatic display, the rapturous cawing of the mutual display in which a united pair stood breast to breast waving their tightly stretched necks from side to side with all the grace and formality of a minuet, twisting and snakelike as if they longed to intertwine in some more satisfying union than their clumsy avian matings allowed.

Sometimes while Forbush watched, silent and forgotten by some sheltering rock, a single bird would begin the lone display, standing straight and graceful as a thrown spear to begin the ecstatic drumming of his throat which acted as a call to the other nest-owners of his colony to stand striving with him. Under this monotonous music—it was harsh and broken like the droning of dark gypsy pipes—the sitting birds would begin the bill-to-flipper display, a low and plaintive feline moaning *warrrraw, warrrraw, warrrraw* slowly in time to the beating flippers of the ecstatic callers and rubbing with ardent beaks their breast feathers first on one side and then on the other as if easing their aching hearts.

Forbush observed the first copulation one warm and sunlit evening as he lay at the top of the slope above Colony 7 with his arms propped on a rock, his chin resting on his wrists. He had stayed languorous and dreaming for an hour or more watching two plump and elegant birds of particular beauty, one lying on a well-built nest, the other standing with hunched shoulders beside, resting but watchful. Every now and then the sitting bird would rise in the nest and the pair would perform a quiet mutual display in which they soundlessly went through their snakelike dance, their open beaks mute yet eloquent, before they changed places. The mountain smoked clear and peaceful, its cloud plume sloping gently down the summit wind, its snowfields pure and smooth.

At last the male bird (Forbush presumed its masculinity for penguins give no outer evidence of sex), bowed its head and began to walk gravely up and down beside its mate.

The hen bird settled comfortably in her hollowed mound, a graceful gondola shape afloat on a timeless stony sea, awaiting without sign of need or desire, without any apparent ripple in the calm of her submissive will, the moment when he stepped carefully on to her shoulders and began a rhythmic treading of her black and downy feathers, his flippers stretched back, edge-down and knifelike to balance his head which now bent down and forwards towards her upward yearning beak so that they met and nuzzled and Forbush heard the gentle click, click and thought he could hear, softly like blood moving in his ears, the beat of the penguin's tread. This became faster, more rhythmic. His beak jabbed downwards at her now, almost savage, as his dancing, drumming feet moved downwards along her broad and rippling back until with tail feathers erect he was poised above her upward strained cloaca. Their contact was so brief, so meagre.

The cold mating of birds. Forbush looked, stared with a stony face and felt his own sex stir deeply within him.

The cock bird stood now before his quiet mate, head bowed, chest slightly puffed. He swallowed several times and hunched his shoulders in sleep.

Forbush slept that night at midnight when the rookery was pale gold and the birds subdued. He dreamed. He picked up a newspaper to look at the weather map and found instead of the usual precise and simple diagram—the two long islands looped about with the great circular air masses that roll across the land from the Southern Ocean—an intricate and beautiful drawing of twisting interwoven lines and carefully balanced areas of shade. Underneath was a statement from the New Zealand Meteorological Service. It said that the weather was so darned fine over the whole country that there was no point in having a weather map that day. Instead the meteorological observers had amused themselves by drawing the most pleasing design they could imagine to express their pleasure in calm weather and here presented it in the hope that their public would be likewise delighted.

Every day Forbush felt more alive. To walk in the

rookery was to feel possessed, almost, of many children whose features slowly became known to him—which bird was placid, which pair rancorous and ill-wed, which pair careful and conscientious in nest-building, which pair scatterbrained and erratic in their preparation for parenthood. These were the golden days before hunger began to affect their ordered lives, before the skuas came to stand watchful on their craggy roosts.

Forbush put up a sign made from a ration box lid lashed to a bamboo marker pole. On it he wrote in rescue-orange paint "Polar Penguin Producers Limited. The Happy Holiday Farm of the Frozen South. Visitors not Welcome. Proprietor R. J. Forbush." This he stuck in a cairn of stones by the lake edge and went about his daily work feeling stirrings of some instinct to husbandry, to till the soil, see things flourish and grow.

Sometimes he would stand on Access Beach, lanky and purposeful with his net, an enlarged butterfly net at the end of a long pole. This he used to capture penguins fresh from the sea ice so that he could daub them with orange paint, amused at their protests and childish wrigglings (the greatest offence seemed to be to their dignity), so that he could follow their course through the rookery to their remembered nest sites.

Later, if they appeared to settle well into colony life he would capture them again and place numbered bands on their flippers. These would be a virtually permanent identification able to be read by binoculars from some distance. His successors at the rookery would be able to follow their breeding progress for years and verify his growing belief that a great proportion of mature adult birds joined the same mate year after year and used the same nest site.

He observed that the reunion of pairs at the nest was not always a straightforward affair. Sometimes a presumed male bird with half-built nest, would accept advances from a female fresh from the sea ice. They would perform the mutual display, the trusting hen would begin stone-gathering as if she was to settle in a permanent home. Then the true wife would arrive. The husband's affection for the paramour would be alienated in a reunion display of great ecstasy and she would be chased squawking from the nest by vindictive blows and pecks from the wedded pair.

"Penguins are dumb," Forbush concluded and pondered on how they could recognise one another when they all looked virtually the same. He discovered that sometimes they did not recognise each other and even became confused about their sex, beginning the procreative act and then transferring roles to conclude it successfully.

He watched with endless interest sometimes sitting in a sheltered corner for eight or ten hours at a time eating chocolate and fruit cake and drinking coffee from a thermos flask when he became stiff and cold. To his amazement some birds seemed to know where their nest lay even if it was covered by snow. They would arrive at the site, peer around with a peculiar swivelling of the head as if they looked first with one eye and then the other. Their first collected stones, absorbing heat from the sun, would melt through the snow in a few hours and their feet would soon trample the nest-mound clear. Fights were frequent, particularly when a mature bird returned to find an inexperienced breeder sitting on his nest. The rightful owner was nearly always successful in chasing the usurper off the nest and out of the colony. It became obvious because rookery life was so strongly territorial that the penguins associated not because they were communal creatures which together formed an organic unit but merely for the protection of numbers and because breeding sites were scarce.

The stones, each one hardly bigger than a hazel nut, seemed to play a prime role in their lives at this time. Without stones the penguins could not incubate their eggs or rear their chicks in the first vulnerable weeks. They provided an air space under the sitting parent which would insulate the eggs from the permanently frozen ground and, later, would raise them clear of melt-water streams which trickled through various parts of the rookery after a blizzard had laid its windrows of drift snow. They also enabled the birds to keep their nests clean. Slowly each nest became ringed with a star-point pattern of excreta which the sitting bird ejected powerfully by contractions of its sphincter muscles. Forbush noted that in every case the excreta was stained green with bile and held no trace of red, the mark of a krill-feeding bird living close to the sea. The penguins had come so far that no food reserves remained in their stomachs. They were now completely reliant on the blubber layers under their skin.

One day he gathered a sackful of stones, painted them all orange and left them in piles in several colonies. A few days later he found coloured stones in practically every nest which showed there was ceaseless movement and competition for the materials of life.

Sometimes birds would walk up to a hundred yards to pick up a stone and run the gauntlet of colony neighbours while trying to carry it, walking with head bent forward and awkward, flippers stretched back, through the rows of sitting birds which pecked, either with malice or simply for the joke of it. Sometimes the stone was lost and the bird, too silly to pick it up again, would begin again his arduous journey.

Some, like the plump male he had watched in the first act of mating, even showed considerable cunning and dissemblement, others a confusion which made Forbush laugh out loud. He watched his happily mated bird sleeping one morning while a lone neighbour laboriously added to his nest, depositing each stone with deliberation and turning to wobble away to his stone supply. Each time he turned the sleeping bird woke; leaned over, hardly shifting his feet, thieved the latest stone and added it to the vast pile on which his hen proudly sat. By the time the builder returned he was asleep again. At the same time two single birds nearby were busily dismantling each others' nests. For twenty minutes they passed each other on a five-yard journey between their respective homes. Each turned his back at the same time to lift a stone from the other's nest. Each one turned on the homeward journey unaware that he had achieved nothing yet glaring at the other suspiciously as they passed. At last one bird got out of phase. He was half-way home while the other was lifting a stone from his nest. *Aaark!* He rushed at the thief, flippers beating and beak wide in outrage. Full of moral certainty, he was an easy winner and performed an indignant display over his nest.

Dissection was the only exact way to tell a bird's sex and Forbush's study demanded data on blubber reserves of birds arriving at the rookery. Feeling like a butcher he went out to take his first bird. In his pocket was a heavy needle set in a wooden handle.

He chose a presumed female a few minutes after she had completed her mating and lifted her from the nest with hardly a flutter holding her carefully away from his body in his leather mittened hands.

"Come on little penguin." He sat on a rock outside her colony still holding her clear of his clothing and pressing her stomach gently so that she ejected excreta. She sat so calmly on his knees while he took the needle out, pressed her head down on his thigh and pushed the needle deftly into the back of her head upwards from the base of her neck, twisting it. She fluttered and stiffened, unmarked.

"How did things change?" Forbush said aloud to the mountain and the sky. "What's the difference?"

As he stood up, swinging the carcass, for that was all it was, by the legs from a suddenly limp hand Forbush saw her mate perform a quiet and graceful display over the empty nest.

On 12 November Forbush found the first egg and returned to the nest a few hours later to see the complete clutch of two. The hen still sat on the eggs, a few hours of maternal peace before she went to sea for food and left her mate to perform the first long patient act of incubation. She would return, if the ice permitted, nearly three weeks later, perhaps a day late or two days. Perhaps never. Perhaps she would return to find nothing of her mating but the guano-stained mound, bare even of stones. The skua gulls, now wheeling and turning over the rookery, high flying and purposeful, hunting low across the lake or crowing their savage challenge from the midnight peaks of black and corroded lava flows, would soon begin to build their nest scoops.

CHAPTER FIVE

"HAVE you ever been in love?"

"Yes—I think so."

"What was it like?"

"It was like a magnet."

"Did it hurt?"

"It consumed me. I wasn't me any longer."

"Did he love you?"

"I never found out."

"Well how did you know you loved him?"

"Because it was like a magnet."

"Why are you so beautiful?"

"At school I was an ugly duckling."

"Did you mind that?"

"Yes—I minded very much and I was determined to become beautiful."

"How could you love him if you didn't know he loved you?"

"Because that's what love is like."

"Is it? Is it?"

"Yes, love is like that. The purest love is the love nobody ever knows."

"How could you bear to love and not be loved?"

"Because I was an ugly duckling."

"Then how did you become beautiful?"

"Because I was proud. My glands helped somewhat."

"Do you mind if I remember you while I'm away?"

"No. I think I might be proud of that too."

"Do you mind if I remember you here like this with my lips on your breast?"

"As long as you don't remember too often."

"Do you mind me looking at you?"

"No. You can look as much as you like. I can give you that at least."

"It's because you are beautiful and I want to remember when I'm gone. Do you mind my hand there?"

"No. It makes me glad you are looking at me."

"I'm going to remember the feel of your arm on the back of my neck and the feel of your hip bones. Do you mind?"

"No. Why are you going? Goodness, I'm trying so hard to look beautiful. Why should I? Why are you going?"

"I don't know. I have a job to do. I don't know. Because life is rich down there. You can dream. It's very simple. You remember things."

"What sort of things?"

"Oh all sorts of things. Things you forgot about years ago. Things when you were very young. Very important things which happened yesterday and you forgot because they hurt. Your sins. The way you hurt people. The way people hurt you—but you can forgive them then—what your mother was like when you were three, what it felt like when your father picked you up, the people you hated at kindergarten, the despair you felt when you were fifteen, the shock of seeing afterbirth in a sheep paddock, of seeing the girl next door had breasts, of winning a race, of first getting drunk, of first standing on top of a mountain, of first swimming out of your depth in the sea. Shush. I want to look at you."

> *Love, you said, is like*
> *The flourishing of flowers*
> *In the heart, unnourished*
> *Except by their own radiance.*

"How did you know you had become beautiful?"

"In a mirror. One day it was there. Nobody told me."

"Have you ever been lonely?"

"Yes."

"What was your most loneliest?"

"Riding a horse in the high country. A windy day. The tussock was all bright with wind. You know how the shingle gleams on a river flat and the water's made of metal. I had a great black horse and I saw a calf being born."

"What's the time?"

"Two o'clock about, I think. Are you tired?"

"No. I wouldn't care if I was. I'll be gone in eighteen hours. In eighteen hours I'll be twenty-five thousand feet high over the Southern Ocean."

"And all you'll have left is dreams."

"I'll still be able to feel you. When I close my eyes I'll feel the touch of your breast in the very centre of the palm of my hand. I'll curl up with my jersey for a pillow and I'll smell the scent of you on it. When I've been away two or three months this will torture me though."

"How do you know? What about your other women?"

"You are erasing them from my mind. There will be no room for any but you."

"Is it very bad—to be without women?"

"Sometimes it's bad. It's a sort of interior thing. A sort of an ache when you're drunk and it's four in the morning. Sunday morning at the end of Saturday night's party and the rum jar's empty and the beer ration's drunk. Outside Mount Erebus is pink like a lollipop because the sun's way down low beyond White Island. The pressure ridges in the sea ice in front of the base are all dark, moving as if the ice was alive. You want to spread out your arms wide and lie on it, cover it, embrace it, make it warm with your own enormous wasted warmth."

"That must be a terrible feeling."

"It's not too bad. You can always go to bed and pretend. I'll remember you."

"I wonder if I'll know, if I'll feel myself being wanted."

"Ha! I don't expect so."

"Don't say that. O don't say that."

"I'm sorry . . . music is worst. I know just the tunes which will make me remember you. I can hear them now, on that scratchy old gramophone we've got down there. I'll play them on my clarinet and I'll feel sick. I won't have much music except what I make because I'll be alone."

"Why will you be alone? Where will you be?"

"At Cape Royds. All summer. Just the birds and the seals and the ice and me. I suppose there'll be people coming and going a bit. It won't be too bad."

"Come closer. Yes. Like that. Now put your arm under

here. And that hand there. Yes. What if I don
you?"

"What a creaky old bed. That won't matter too much,
suppose. After all, you'll be in the world. You've got to go
on living just the same. It's only me who'll be isolated."

"But supposing I do miss you. What if I long for you all
the time?"

"Then I suppose you'll wait."

"But what if you've changed when you come back—a
whole summer's change?"

"I've never known whether things changed in a summer
or not, whether the earth was different at the end of it."

"That's no answer."

"How can I answer?"

"Come closer. Why haven't you kissed me?"

"I don't know. I feel as if this is one long kiss. This.
There's so little time that this is timeless. Time doesn't
mean anything. There's plenty of time."

"Kiss me then."

"I'll remember this. I'll go on the rack for it."

"Kiss me then."

"Yes."

"Will you remember that kiss?"

"Yes. The world I'm going to is so bitter and so fine. It's
a place for great thoughts and ideals but hardly anybody
who goes there has them any more. Look. Thank you for
this. Thank you for this. Every man is alone there locked
up with his own dreams, his otherlife, his otherworld.
Sometimes you try and share, sometimes you feel you've
got to share, to tell, but it really doesn't work. It's so bitter
there sometimes, so black and white, so definite and un-
ambiguous. We're so used to ambiguity. We live in an ambiguous colourful world. But there—there's only black and
white, the colours of air and water. I'm so glad I'm going to
be alone, unambiguously alone. Kiss me."

"Yes. Look. I'm yours now. Quickly. Come on. Quickly.
While there's time. While I'm yours. Yes. Yes. Do that. Oh
do that. I'm yours. Quickly."

he languid tide of love pours
ound my skin, draws in sweet haste
rom my heart the first strong course
Of blood so that I lie open
And golden for your taste.

When he left her the morning was soft with mist from the river, a cool misty green spring morning. The great scarlet flowers of a rhododendron tree lay squashed on the pavement by the gate, glistening like torn pieces of flesh. Wide-eyed at the lightening sky he stopped at an all-night petrol station to telephone a taxi.

The skua gulls were courting. Towards the last week of November the first strident male laid his claim to a territory in the penguin rookery and began to issue his regular challenge—the warlike scream, *Kaaa. Kaaa. Kaaa. Kaaa. Kaaa*, delivered with the head proudly raised and chest thrust forward, wide open beak with its cruelly curved upper mandible, one foot defiantly in front of the other, wings fanned and raised upwards to display his splendid white, black and rich brown feathers. After each day's egg count—each day took longer for the laying had well begun—Forbush spent his watch in the rookery trying to discover how the skuas divided up their territories.

By the end of the month it was clear that only six pairs of birds held rookery territory and another dozen or so would nest on the Cape but forage outside the rookery. Forbush took a map of the Cape out with him each day and slowly drew in the boundaries of each pair's claim. The skuas went to great lengths to prevent stray birds from encroaching on their land. Day long the air rang with their strident challenges clearly heard even above the penguins' din. When each pair formed the male skua began the courtship feeding he would be forced to continue until the eggs were hatched.

It was at this time that Forbush first became aware of his hatred for the skuas. The emotion was alarming because it conflicted with his pride in scientific objectivity. Later in the season he could not even remember when he had first felt it but always came to equate it with the hen skua's vicious and continuing demands for food from a mate who was driven constantly to kill, to forage, to steal from the rookery and even to fly, ceaselessly, the weary miles between rookery and sea and back laden with fish, his head and breast helmeted in ice from the spray of his fishing.

When the cock skua returned from such foraging he would alight with that same massive and controlled braking beat of pinions that Forbush had observed on the misty day when he saw the first bird of the spring. He would land always some distance from the ridge-top nest and the hen would come running over the rocks, insatiable craw stretched tight as she ran with head thrust out, beak open, wings hunched, screeching her demand. The cock would try to disgorge his burden of fish, some more than six inches long, before the hen reached him and began pecking his head and throat, beating with her wings in a frenzy of hunger. Forbush wondered if it was only hunger which made her display so much violence of need. He hated her rapacity and feared for his penguins yet grudgingly admired the skuas for their strength of purpose, the fury and action with which they manifested their survival.

It was to this growing frenzy of food gathering, this appearance of lust to kill and feed (though Forbush told himself there was no lust, only a will to survival, no greed for food, for the sweet orange yolk of penguin eggs, the salty blood of a dead bird in the brief minutes before its carcass froze, but only the need to stay alive), that the last of the breeding penguins waddled in over the ice and set up their homes. Last summer with the sea only two miles distant there had been an estimated 1600 nesting pairs of birds at the first peak of the season. This summer the rookery was beginning with 1139 nests. Last summer about 1800 chicks erupted from their shells. How many this summer?

The skua gulls were bold—only six pairs of them and a thousand penguins, and yet the shadow of their flight across each colony showed itself as an apprehensive ripple of upward turned heads, peering eyes, nervous beaks, among the tight groups of sitting penguins. After each silent pass was over, the skua gliding or drifting, its quick head all alert, the penguins would settle uneasily over their clutches of two white eggs or stand in the nest to perform the display of possession, bending their heads down to rake the eggs protectively under their breasts, between their legs against the featherless scar of warm skin from which the eggs obtained most incubating heat.

Or the skuas would sit watchful on some rock, even the hen birds discarding reliance on their mate's foraging now that food was available on their territory. It was all so quiet, Forbush thought, as he watched the delicate flight of a skua which landed briefly in the thick of a small colony to snatch up an egg rolled from the nest of a nervous parent. The skua flew to clear ground, dropped the egg, crowed its fierce and defiant challenge and then, with deft blows of its beak, cracked a hole in the shell to sip carelessly at the yolk within. The penguins made no attempt to protect the egg. It was abandoned. Nobody owned it once it lay beyond that untidy mound of stones on which it had been laid. They only leaned on their eggs and hissed their hatred at the skua.

Forbush looked with dread to the day when the daily count of eggs, carefully recorded, colony by colony, four pencilled "ones" with the fifth to cross them out, would reach its upper limit and then begin to decline. The harsh and echoless challenge of the skuas was the last sound he heard as he went to sleep at night and the first he heard in the morning because a pair had made their nest beside a lava pinnacle behind the hut and when he went to the drift bank for water snow they screamed and dived at him.

Each time he saw the last egg laid in a clutch and the penguin pair begin the ceremony of changing places on the nest he felt a slight and depressing tremor of despair. What were the chances, how did the odds stand today, this day when the sun was high, the ice white and blinking towards the horizonless north? What hope was there for these eggs, for this now thin and tired hen penguin who was shuffling off the nest and performing a solemn mutual display with her mate who shuffled on to the eggs, tucked them carefully under his breast and prepared for his long and bitter fast of incubation? The hen usually stood beside her mate an hour or two in silent communion, sadly bowing her head, it seemed. Then she would gather stones, a last service or a last rite. She would be gone seventeen, eighteen, nineteen days, at least that, weeks of striving to return, fat from the sea with a full craw to feed her chicks. He would wait, wait, wait, every day a little weaker, a little less warm, a little hungrier, already having wasted so much on those dogged seventy-five miles of hard-blue ice. Could he wait?

She would walk away at last, picking her path carefully and with growing purpose through her colony neighbours, over the bare stony ground, over the guano and old bones, the shrunken carcasses of past summers, down to the beach. If she stood there alone she would wait a few hours until three or four other birds weak with the release of laying joined her. They would set off then, together in a straggling line, northwards towards the sea, the bright blue water which Forbush could see in his mind but could not hear.

Each time he saw a group leave he felt he had to stand in some sort of ineffectual farewell salute. "God speed, fair winds, or something. I don't know."

At the peak of laying there were 1217 eggs in the rookery. Six hundred less than last summer, perhaps eight hundred less by the time the hatching came, a thousand less at the first week of chick rearing, 1200 less at the end of the first month. Less and less, and how many tireless summers to go, how many endless cycles of birth and death on this stony Cape? How could they exist, continue?

As the rookery settled to the sleepy silence of incubation and the rhythm of the days lengthened Forbush found himself imbued with the same patience. Life became reflective. He remembered things, just as he had told Barbara he would remember. His sense of contact with the past was so strengthened that there no longer seemed anything bizarre about living in his tidy corner of the old hut. He tried to discipline his life against the unending day, to keep regular hours, going to sleep about midnight each night and waking before nine in the morning. Morning after morning he rose, cooked breakfast, washed dishes, counted eggs, sat at vantage points in the rookery until mid-afternoon, ate a light lunch, washed dishes and returned to the rookery to kill for dissection, band flippers, take photographs, weigh and measure eggs and incubating parents. By seven o'clock he would be inside the hut again cooking dinner, the endless compressed meat-bar stew now that his fresh meat was consumed but for a couple of chickens and some kidneys carefully stored for Christmas.

Some nights, like the night he had remembered that long conversation with Barbara, unreal and beautiful, in her flat, in her bed, he would lie on top of his sleeping bag for hours staring at the shadowy ceiling or out through the window and up at the crag on which the hen skua crouched both nestling and alert. He remembered things, heard conversations again, standing outside himself and looking on, looking down at himself with faint and fond amusement, hearing the words writhe upwards from the moving lips of his characters so that they wreathed and twined about him like smoke. He would feel secure, needed by his past, as if it was all still taking place and could not be completed without his participation.

"God I'm depressed. You know I really am in a terrible depressive state," he would suddenly say aloud and decide to go to bed immediately. He tried to think of amusing projects for evening diversion like writing a satirical paper postulating and, of course, proving the egg theory of human fertility which holds that it is really men who have children. They simply deposit them in egg form in the female womb where they are incubated until the moment of hatching or birth. This hypothesis had always intrigued him illustrating, as it did, the obvious power and dignity of man.

Sometimes he spent hours peering at his face in his tiny steel mirror removing blackheads with surgical competence and precision and then trimming his beard with nail scissors with the aim of providing himself with a perfectly summetrical face on which not one sprouting hair was more than three thousandths of an inch too long or too short. Such activity usually only reminded him that there was nobody to trim his beard for, anyway, which depressed him so that he had again to retire to bed.

On other nights he risked the waning power of his radio

batteries to eavesdrop on the noises the world was making. He enjoyed particularly the Voice of the Andes and its religious propaganda for he could get so enraged that he could run outside and try to smash the ice on the edge of Pony Lake with enormous lava boulders seized and hurled while he jumped up and down shouting "Fools, sycophantic nincompoops, blind idiots" as the American voice drawled on, quivering with inspiration and certainty. Forbush swore at the skuas and threw stones until they screamed back at him. Then he could go inside, turn off the radio and make himself a soothing cup of cocoa.

His greatest triumph was the Penguin Major Polyphonic Music Machine. This proved to be a long-term project capable of endless modification and extension. Forbush had invented the Penguin Minor Polyphonic Music Machine by mistake one night while he was playing his clarinet (*Basin Street Blues* complete with improvised variations in diminished time) and warming his bare and dirty toes on the table beside the roaring Primus. Presently he discovered that he had picked up a fork between the big and second toe of his right foot and was beating it in time on the Primus tank. He discovered this because his big toe was getting too hot and then found that his left toes were curled round his dried penguin's foot and were scraping it on a billy lid so that it produced a low-frequency squeak which was not unpleasant or out of keeping with his fork banging and clarinet blowing. He augmented the time of his tune and deftly lengthened his clutch on the fork to increase the distance between toes and heat.

This was not strictly a machine, he was forced to admit, but later, when the inspired construction of the Penguin Major was under way he decided that his initial discovery should be dignified with such a title. The construction began with that blind, intuitive, apparently directionless yet daemonically purposeful collection of materials which characterises all great inventions. Forbush had always believed in serendipity, the art of making discoveries, by accident and sagacity, of things you are not in quest of (he was convinced that his major contributions to science would be revealed in such a way) and began his work in faith. That his aim was vague, his purpose ill-defined and his chance of success utterly remote did not discourage him. Discoveries like the sudden revelation that Alphonse the rabbit squeaked when pressed delighted him and strengthened his belief in the infallible creative workings of his inner mind. One night when he was a little drunk on his second to last weekly ration of beer he reeled slightly against the curtain which Alphone straddled, knocked him on to the floor and stood on him. Alphonse squeaked and Forbush was inspired.

He worked feverishly for several hours abandoning for the moment his planning of the basic instrument of the P.Ma.P.M.M.—a water-bottle xylophone made from Shackleton's sauce bottles and Professor T. Edgeworth David's mouldering test tubes—to construct a foot-operated Alphonse squeaker. This operation had its problems, for Alphonse had to be secured to his mount (a member of the machine the design of which had to incorporate a means of attachment to the xylophone because Forbush was determined that the P.Ma.P.M.M. should be portable) so firmly that he could not be dislodged in playing or transport, and yet not so firmly that his stomach was depressed to the extent that he was unable to gulp sufficient air to allow him to squeak.

Some timber from Shackleton's historic horse-stalls would not be missed, Forbush was sure, and he duly found suitable lengths of weathered board which in their desiccated state could easily be chopped and broken into Alphonse-size pieces. First he tried lashing the rabbit to a base board with meteorological balloon cord thoughtfully stolen from the met shack at McMurdo Station before he left Scott Base, but was forced to admit that it did not work. Each time he pressed his bare toes into Alphonse's stomach Alphonse was displaced slightly on the board and three times out of five refused to squeak. With a sigh Forbush realised he must face up to the demands of his genius and construct a more complex instrument on which he could keep accurate time.

The solution proved to be a box with one open end skilfully fashioned from the sides of a British Antarctic Expedition 1906 ration box and tacked together with its rusty

staples. On to this Alphonse was impaled by ears and feet.
The final subtle refinement was a thicker and more durable
piece of horse-stall timber fashioned into a foot pedal and
hinged, alas, with wire from Shackleton's toaster. Forbush
felt a twinge of guilt. He pushed the pedal with his bare
right toes. Alphonse squeaked. He played a Dixie version of
September in the Rain and Alphonse squeaked ecstatically
right through.

Forbush awoke the next day tinged with remorse. How
far would his new preoccupation lead him along the path of
vandalism and desecration of a historic monument of which
he was the sole custodian and only visitor? He realised that
the construction of the P.Ma.P.M.M. would be a bitter-
sweet endeavour and yet felt driven on, forced towards total
involvement with his inventive passion while dark clouds of
guilt gathered over the bright day when he would give his
first concert. He decided that at least he should abandon
construction for a day, deny himself until he was forced to
continue at a time when guilt was assuaged by virtuous
feelings at having held out for so long.

The day was bright. No wind again. Fair weather and
calm now seemed the natural state of the earth after so
many days had passed without any apparent change in the
landscape except for the slow diminution of snowdrifts
round the hut and rookery, not yet a melting decay but a
continuing evaporation which passed unnoticed until a new
rock or rubbish pile was revealed.

He walked slowly across the lake, the rookery and down
to Access Beach, then over the tide crack and out across
the ice, past the stranded growler and the ice hummock to
stand in the high warm sun looking back at his homeland
and the mountain. The ice on which he stood seemed just
as permanent, just as solid and impregnable to the sea until
he saw the seal. She lay beside a crack at the north end of
the beach and he could not understand why he had not seen
her before. As he watched, the little grey pup at her side
flicked his hind-quarters into the air and clapped his hands
to the sun.

That was how it looked to Forbush—as if the seal pup
was suddenly aware of its life and the joy of its kicking

limbs, as if its blood had stirred with the new season and pounded forcefully for a moment in its veins so that it waved its forelimbs in recognition of being alive.

"How does it know? O it must be so aware of itself. How does it feel the difference?" Forbush asked as he walked close enough to see the pup's soft grey fur, its velvet skin still too big for its body and almost draped round its neck, its enormous round black eyes innocent and unblinking. The pup bounced its skinny buttocks hard on the ice three times and then raced wriggling in the undulant crawl of Weddell seals right round its mother and back again to look at Forbush with snow crystals on its wiffling nose.

"How did you get here?" Forbush asked the seal which lay like a great mottled cigar on the shallow depression her warmth and ordure had hollowed in the ice. She scratched her scarred chest slowly with a clawed flipper. There was no obvious hole, no milky-green melt pool of salty slush through which she might have risen.

"Something must be happening, the ice must be easing to have let you through. Surely it can't be long now."

CHAPTER SIX

THERE was an obvious reason, friends had once told Forbush, to explain why he had become an ornithologist. He had been named after Richard John Seddon ("King Dick"), the great politician of the days of New Zealand's emergence as a nation and of whom a verdigris-tinged and warrior-like statue stood in the grounds of Parliament House, Wellington. This statue was almost always surmounted by a resting sea gull, indicating R.J.'s continuing affinity for birds. His hair was all white with guano, a dripping avian tribute to his worth and valour. Thus, Forbush was told by his friends, was established the nexus between fame and ornithology which led him unerringly to the frozen south.

Always sensitive he was inclined to regard this as a cruel jibe because he was really very proud of his Antarctic experience. In any case he was not a mere ornithologist. His concern was with the great problems which confronted life science. He was no mere anatomist or taxonomist, he would say, and at least he knew something about music and literature. "You've got to be integrated these days. Science can be so limited." And then to himself, "Damn—why do I take it all so seriously?"

Yet uncertainty plagued him. One of his favourite quotations was from a general account of the state of modern biology which he had read early in his degree course—"the source of uncertainty is of momentous importance", words that now preyed on his mind enlarged in meaning far beyond their scientific context which had merely drawn attention to the fact that in any measurement or experiment there were hidden unknowns and uncertainties created solely by the practical and material problems of measurement and experiment, and always ready to confound the most carefully calculated conclusions. If science was a forest of uncertainties life itself was a veritable thorn thicket and even his simple, closely prescribed existence at Cape Royds was hedged about with more perplexing unknowns than he had ever before become aware of.

Dimly he realised that the greatest uncertainty of all was death. He lived with it as the weeks drew on towards Christmas and it manifested itself daily with growing frequency. And this he realised, was merely the death of the germ of life in the eggs the skuas daily cracked and sipped, death here concerned itself only with ceasing the replication of protein molecules in the turbulent yolks. Death had so light a touch, a few minutes only of bitter cold would kill a deserted clutch of eggs without the stabbing blows of the skua's beak. Aware that life triumphed here by sheer weight of numbers—there was always something left in the reservoir of convulsing, replicating cells no matter how harsh the ice, how cruel the blizzard or how bold the skua—Forbush yet felt the theft of life from every single egg as a blow against the philosophy of individualism in which he instinctively believed, as a wound in his soul beleaguered as it was by the forces of corporateness and of personal insignificance. Again and again he had to tell himself of the skuas, "It's not their fault. They are simply another force in the total complex of forces which make up life. It doesn't matter what happens to the eggs. They are still part of life. Life is immutable. To talk of 'dead' or 'alive' is meaningless."

He hated the skuas. When the eggs hatched they would eat the chicks.

Daily the desertion of nests grew more frequent and a general feeling of anxiety seemed to affect the whole rookery. The incubating male birds did not have the resources to continue their fast. They were no longer the shining and clean, plump and determined little creatures that had appeared out of the ice-blink a month ago. They were thin, their head feathers always, it seemed to Forbush, erect and angular. Their breasts were stained with bile-green guano and their leg feathers dingy with mud and dust. The strong stench of fishy excrement, ammoniac and choking, which hung over the rookery was like the stench of despair and seemed tangible.

Moody and depressed Forbush began his first twenty-four-hour watch. He filled his pack with a thermos of coffee and one of soup, hard sledging biscuits, a tin of butter and one precious tin of beer, with binoculars, camera, notebook and pencil, sleeping bag and eiderdown jacket and trudged out to his favourite lookout on the Cape. It was three o'clock in the afternoon and the sun was high over Beaufort Island. Mount Erebus hardly smoked and was surely not itself decaying in this dreary summer? By midnight Forbush had seen seven penguins desert their nests and fourteen eggs devoured by the skuas, which no longer flew over the colonies but sat watching silently from strategic rocks.

He tried to discover if there were any signs by which he might tell when a nest was going to be deserted but there was no indication until the bird slowly and cumbersomely rose from the eggs, pecked at them, then stood to one side peering at them, the movements of its head and neck hinting at the forgotten passion of the mutual display. It would appear to sleep a while with hunched shoulders standing over the eggs. With a final offering of stones to the nest, placed so deliberately as if they were appointed guardians of the eggs, a position of trust conferred with utter faith, the penguin would turn and walk slowly to the beach. It would not look back. Far north over the ice Forbush could see the retreating black backs.

At midnight when the sun was high and he sat cosy with his down jacket round his shoulders and his sleeping bag drawn over his legs up to his waist Forbush dozed and dreamed.

He lay hidden in some flax bushes on the burial hill above the headland at the entrance to Torrent Bay. The flax leaves hissed and rattled faintly with every shudder of wind. He saw a gannet dive, dropping like a spear from fifty feet to hit the sea with hardly a splash. In the shadowy stillness of water beside Totara Reef he saw a giant stingray flap slowly between two weedy crags and the small fish go to ground in its path. The sun was bright in his eyes and on the satin flax leaves which rattled like arrows in a quiver. Away east and north across the breadth of Tasman Bay he could see the dim blue bulk of D'Urville Island and the hills of Marlborough where the South Island ran under the sea.

There was a ship in Torrent Bay working her way carefully, with topsails aback and slatting, through the patches of white water where the sea groaned on a reef. There was no sound from the people standing on the yellow sands below him. They were as stiff and silent as the canoes drawn up above the tide and lying dark, oval and symmetrical, shaped like the taut smiles of mouths stretched in death.

The ship, so tall and gracious that she seemed bigger than the land itself, that delicate land where the fragrant bush bent down to touch a tidal shore, and so indomitable with her salt-grey sails and the sun gleaming on her white gunports, stopped then and swung head to wind and sea obedient to her anchor. The anchor had splashed without a sound. The sails were furled and the yards braced with no creak of running rigging, squeak of a block or laboured shouts of men.

The sun on the leaves of flax almost blinded Forbush and he did not believe he saw a morepork, the night owl, sitting on the dried brown stalk of flax flower in front of him. The morepork clawed its way higher on the stalk, which waved and bent with the weight, so that black and waxy seeds from the swollen pads were shaken on to the mossy soil and over his naked legs.

Morepork, said the morepork and Forbush, whose sight was filled with golden blindess did not believe it spoke. "*Morepork*. It's too late. They've come at last, you see. In a hundred years my people will be gone from here and yours will seldom come. Between their coming I shall know peace but never the same peace of laughter round the cooking pits, the nose flute singing in the moonlight from this hill."

The sun went behind a cloud and Forbush found his sight and was chilled. He shifted his hips on the hard lava stones and poured soup from his thermos. Two skuas sped past his roost in marvellous, flashing flight, a trespasser pursued.

Every hour he wrote notes on his observations — the number of nest desertions and the behaviour of deserting birds; the time lapse between desertion and theft of the eggs by skuas, flight paths of skuas over the Cape, frequency of egg-turning and displays by marked birds in nearby colonies, numbers of non-breeding and yearling penguins now beginning to arrive from the sea and their behaviour on arrival, air temperature taken with a hand-whirled thermometer, the frequency and duration of sleep periods by sitting birds.

It was hard not to sleep. At four o'clock in the morning a scrawny yearling penguin wandered up to his camp and said *Aark* three times belligerently, its flippers stretched out stiffly like a schoolboy yelling "Ya boo!" Forbush threw a pebble. It scuttled away but turned round twenty feet distant to say *Aark*, in a jeering catch-me-if-you-can voice. Forbush laughed out loud and the sun was high over White Island, distant in the south. He had never felt so completely and terribly alone.

It was not the loneliness of panic, of lost love, of being single in a multitude or the terrible ecstasy of being alone in a night composed only of stars. It became, quite suddenly, the sick loneliness of creatures abandoned by their kind. Fox, wolf, jackal, hyena, coyote, he felt all of these—alone and outcast, a wanderer, padding silently through forests without meaning, deserts of silence, the dry watercourses of despair. The sickness of being alone knotted his stomach, swelled in his throat, made his limbs nerveless as if the courses of normal feeling were attenuated round his heart. His mouth was full of the acrid taste of bile. With stiff fingers he felt his arms, his legs, the stringy muscles of his back, the taut cords of his stomach and the fretting sinews of his thighs. His skin was like bark, as hard and as rough, over the sluggish flow of his blood. "The earth is so chill. My roots are contracting and dying," he thought. A skua called his savage challenge from a distant rock.

"O grass. Warm sunshine. What does warm grass smell like in the evening after each blade has curled and melted under the day of sun?" Forbush closed his eyes against the ice.

Grass. Tree. Bird. Fish. Water. Horse. Stag. Tussock. Hen. Boat. Pavement. Magnolia. Clematis. Red wine. Celery. Weed. Bus. Garden. Paddock. Sheep. Sunburn. Sand. Tide pool. Surf swim. Willow. Moon. Star. Green. Shorts. Silk. Bare feet. River. Flower. House. O warm, O peace.

The words had a strange brilliance, an impact which

made him shiver and slide gently and luxuriously with arms clasped round his chest deep into his sleeping bag. He shivered, not with cold, and it was again almost as if she had just touched his back, her light fingers running once down the serrations of his backbone, between his shoulders at the moment when he had first become aware of her. Later he said it was as if he was breathing her into himself with every deep breath but then, only twenty-four hours before he climbed on an immense rumbling aeroplane to fly south, when they were still looking at each other, covertly, with great curiosity, she had made him utterly aware of herself with just one light touch.

This was one, yes, two, three, yes, four hours after they met at dinner, the last entertainment, at the home of his professor. She was a librarian, yes, a university librarian.

"Goodness. Do you enjoy that?" (She was much too attractive.)

"Yes—I think so." (The raised eyebrow over the rim of the glass. Why does she only think so?)

"Barbara majored in English, Dick. We thought you'd have so little in common you'd find each other interesting."

"Oh really?" His best imitation of American conversational punctuation. Laughter. Pause. The other eyebrow raised. The secret smile. Listening to the faint, delicate, almost fragrant (he thought then in that flower-filled room with that very iced drink stinging his finger tips) music of Mozart on the gramophone. "I know you think we're all under-educated, sir, but I'm glad you imply some recognition of our native wit." (The professor was English. Find each other interesting!)

"It's . . . it's rather early yet. Would you like to have coffee somewhere?" They had escaped. The night was warm and damp with mist. Damn. Damn. Damn tomorrow. Why must I go tomorrow?

After that they went dancing, of all things, at a little coffee and dance place where a blind Maori sat playing jazz on a piano and the drummer was a seedy thin man whose brittle face cracked with the joy of his drumming every now and then and the saxophonist was fat and sweating in a bow tie which drooped on both sides. Sometimes the fat man played the double bass and sometimes he got carried away and beat wildly on the cymbals while everybody shook and danced and shuffled and twisted and shuddered and jerked and panted and smiled to themselves and grinned and bit their tongues in apparent Bacchic frenzy while the blind Maori played implacably as if the piano was an incongruous growth sprouting from his fingertips and feet, itself jiving and bouncing and quivering to the music which came pouring into the room as if from a celestial agency lighting with joy the thin man and the fat man and the drums, cymbals, double bass, saxophone, blind Maori, piano, coffee cups, rickety tables, untidy ashtrays, crude murals on the walls, tattered bead curtains and the radiant faces of the dancers. They hardly noticed because at that moment Barbara's fingers touched Forbush's serrated backbone between the shoulderblades so that he shivered and felt a tremor in his heart and thighs (together and at once, he realised, appalled) and they stopped dancing to clasp each other very tight and close in the middle of the floor. O God why am I going away?

Later, whenever he got scared at the thought of having to leave her he told himself it was better that way. Why, there'd be no time to grow sick of each other. At the end of twenty-four hours almost continuously together they would know each other inside out, probably, and it would be a good thing that he was going. It would save him from getting bored.

The men stood in the long S curve from the airport terminal building to the tail door of the Globemaster. The animals went in two by two. It was dark with the strange, blue runway lights silhouetting the aircraft and its bright orange tail. Earlier, in the evening calm, a Super Constellation had drifted down over the runway like a silver and orange dragon. These blue lights were dragonfire.

He'd lost her in the panic of the call for final briefing in the terminal lounge when an American Navy lieutenant-commander had stood up on a chair and bellowed at them to answer their names and told them to make sure they found the life jackets and survival suits under the hummocky webbing seats lining the walls of the cargo compartment in the plane. He'd lost her because he had to run dragging his kitbags like dead drunken bodies across the lounge carpet to the dim-lit doors. He'd lost her after one frantic glance behind and couldn't even wave or leap up to try to see her over the other people's heads. Then the Globe-master had swallowed him up.

After midnight he had looked out through the window to see the pale draped gold of an aurora and feel its coldness. He crawled into a miraculously empty canvas bunk but had to lie on his stomach otherwise his hipbone heaved on the bulging bum of the man in the bunk above him. The whole cargo deck of the Globemaster throbbed and roared while he buried his head in his rolled up jersey finding that it con-tained her fragrance and he could breathe her into himself, still, in great aching breaths.

He couldn't sleep. The stones were too hard and cold under his hips.

The rookery was waking or rather the rhythm of its life seemed to be quickening as the sun began to roll upwards on its course towards noon. Forbush opened his can of beef and ate thick slabs between buttered sledging biscuits that were too sweet and crumbly. They had been prepared to a recipe devised by women in the domestic science faculty of a New Zealand university.

"I was very hungry. That was the trouble," he told himself as he munched and scanned the rookery, eyes squinting against the glare of light from the ice of Pony Lake.

It seemed as though he had always been sitting out in the rookery, as if this was his home, his pile of stones, his nest. Each hour he wrote his notes, stood up and stretched to take the temperature. At eight o'clock Bird No. 197 in Colony 14 had a fight with a non-breeding wanderer which had tried to steal stones after sitting in the colony for half an hour with-out winking a dissembling eye. The wanderer was fresh from the sea and persistent. The fight knocked two neighbour birds off their nests and 197's eggs rolled out of their nest and down through the rows of birds and the steep colony slope. A skua was waiting at the bottom almost as if it knew the eggs would come right to its feet. Its mate grabbed one egg from one of the disturbed nests but the other was saved by an enraged and hissing parent.

At nine o'clock, when all was quiet except for the rattling of stones in the nearest colony as a penguin scratched a depression in its nest mound with paddling back legs, the man with the red bathing suit descended out of the sky.

He was a short fat man with a big nose and tortoise-shell rims on his glasses. He was very polite, almost obsequious and certainly reverent towards Forbush.

That he perpetrated an outrage was hardly his fault. In fact it was the fault of a public relations man in Oceanville who gave him the red bathing suit. To anybody from Oceanville it was like somebody from New York giving somebody who was going to the South Pole a little bottle which could be filled with snow which would turn to water and could be brought back to New York so that the somebody could water the window boxes in his penthouse with real Antarctic water and see whether or not the plants died. Just as exciting.

Forbush had been sleeping soundly when he woke, startled, to see a helicopter landing on the pad behind the hut. He had leapt up and sprinted through the rookery, sliding across the lake.

"Mr. Forbush I think it's the most wonderful thing to meet somebody who's actually living, actually living in one of these historic huts. I mean it's practically a monument," said the short fat man whose name was Joe Sloberman. "Gee a monument, that's wonderful, Mr. Forbush, that's wonderful."

The husky sincerity of his voice and his humble, downcast eyes deeply affected Forbush who found himself standing on one leg rubbing the tattered toe of his other mukluk into the gravel.

"You don't know how grateful I'd be, Mr. Forbush, if you'd just let me take your picture standing over there, yes that's right Mr. Forbush, this'll only take a minute. Just there by that rugged old door. Yes. Yes. Hold it thank you. Hold it. Thank you Mr. Forbush, I can't thank you enough."

Standing stiffly to attention, his hairy chin buried in his anarak, his woolly hat pulled over his ears and his eyes closed behind his snowglasses Forbush nearly went to sleep again.

"Damn. Hallucinations. I shouldn't have tried a twenty-four-hour watch. Must sleep." H swayed on his feet. Silence.

"Ahem . . . er . . . Mr. Forbush, do you think we might have a look inside your hut now?"

Forbush opened his eyes incredulously. There were eight of them—Al Weiser and another man in orange and six others, who all looked exactly alike in bulky U.S. Army cold weather clothing, standing with legs apart and monkeylike arms dangling, necks slung with cameras and fists stuck into heavy mitts hanging from tape harness over their shoulders, fur-lined hoods valiantly pulled up. They looked like silhouettes from a pictorial population graph and Forbush searched for the half man at the end of the row, disturbed to find he was not there.

"Why hello, Dick Forbush I presume." One of the monkey men stepped forward and extended a monkey hand. "I hope you'll excuse us dropping in on your little camp like this well I'm John Smith Cranford Junior, Lieutenant U.S.N. Public Information officer at McMurdo Station and I've just brought these people over to have a look at the little penguins and we want to have a look at your little hut here too say I guess you're pretty comfortable in there Mr. Forbush do you mind if we take a look around gentlemen this is Mr. Dick Forbush Mr. Forbush I'd like you to meet Evan Jenkins of the *Harrisburg Enquirer* Mr. Forbush David Goldthwaite of the *San Francisco Post* and *Star* Mr. Forbush Judge Coxfoot of Nathan County Massachusetts Mr. Forbush Acharya Prabhavananda of the *Journal of India* Mr. Forbush Konstantin Kirsanov of *Pravda* Mr. Forbush and Joe Sloberman of the *Oceanville Citizen-Journal* Mr. Forbush . . ."

"We've met," interjected Joe Sloberman humbly and shook Forbush's quivering hand with a hand which was plump and soft.

". . . Well Dick I reckon you'd be just the person to show us round this old hut of yours . . ."

"Oh Mr. Forbush we'd be delighted so delighted," interjected Joe Sloberman and Forbush felt his jaws stiffen with smiling his welcome smile and his neck beginning to ache from nodding his head.

"Step right in gentlemen step right in its only a small place but it's all mine you know all mine." Forbush felt he should say "Tee Hee" and skip. Calm yourself Forbush, calm yourself ohmygod the Penguin Major Polyphonic Music Machine not to mention the dirty dishes.

He led the way inside and having been told that in Antarctica they must always walk in the footsteps of the man in front because if they strayed off the path they might fall in a crevasse they followed him silent and in single file with cautious tread across the snow-drifts round the door.

He showed them Shackleton's stove ("Gee that's great Mr. Forbush you can almost smell that old seal blubber cooking away"), Shackleton's bed ("Just think of the lonely hours that great man must have spent on that very bed Mr. Forbush why that's marvellous"), Shackleton's sledge ("I really admire the English Mr. Forbush gee those were great men Mr. Forbush great men when you think what they went through . . ."), the holes in Shackleton's dirty old socks ("Yeah this place must sure be tough on the feet Mr. Forbush trudging over all that snow"), Shackleton's sauce bottle and tinned plum duff ("To think they even had pickled mushrooms down here in those days well gee that's great you won't go hungry in here eh Mr. Forbush *and* horseradish sauce!")

"And what were all those bottles and test tubes for Mr. Forbush?"

"Tragic, tragic," muttered Forbush.

"Go on! Go on!" Joe Sloberman almost shrieked, his eyes shining like raisins.

"A pathetic piece of polar history," said Forbush deeply committed and overcome with guilt.

Acharya Prabhavananda stepped cautiously forward peering from under his fur-lined hood and stretched a reverent brown hand towards a bottle of mouldy pickled onions.

"What's that, what's that, what's he saying," said elderly Judge Coxfoot shuffling close. Even Pravda's jaw dropped and Evan Jenkins raised a supercilious eyebrow.

"That . . . that . . . my friends is the last pathetic project undertaken by the renowned Captain Scott and his great friend Dr. Wilson." Forbush sighed deeply from embarrassment interpreted as deep emotion. "Before they left on their last journey these two great friends were engaged in constructing a water-bottle xylophone."

"A water-bottle xylophone?"

"A water-bottle xylophone. Music was their great solace."

"And you mean . . . these old bottles and things . . . this was going to be a water-bottle xylophone?"

"That is so. This pathetic collection of old bottles was going to become Antarctica's first native musical instrument. It was a great project."

"I think that's the saddest thing I've ever seen," Joe Sloberman said.

"It's very sad," said Forbush. "They died before they could complete it."

"I thought their hut was at Cape Evans," said Evan Jenkins.

"Oh . . . er . . . they commuted . . . they had to have somewhere quiet to work. You know how it is Mr. Jenkins oh I mean it's not so far to come you know. And it was spring time so they could wander up over the ice. Anyway they wanted to surprise the men."

"I think that's the saddest thing I've ever seen," said Joe Sloberman.

"Yes well gentlemen now perhaps you'd like to sign the Visitors' Book. It's just right over here on the stove and I'm quite sure your pilot Mr. Weiser here doesn't want his helicopter to get cold and there's other things to see outside you know, there's the dog kennel and the horse-stalls, bits of old motor-car you know and the lavatory seat, that's still there, wait a moment wait a moment I think I've got a pencil ah yes here you are we must have all your signatures in the Visitors' Book of course you'd like to be first Judge wouldn't you I'm sure. The weather doesn't look too good anyway . . . does it?"

Nobody moved. They just keep staring at me, Forbush thought wildly. What's wrong with me anyway.

"Well come on Cranford where's this Visitors' Book?" said the Judge and shuffled towards the stove.

"This is the greatest day of my life," Joe Sloberman told Forbush as they gathered round the stove. "The greatest. Do you know that I've been longing to get down here ever since I was nine years old. Nine years old! I've read all the books you know. All of them, I've read them, but they don't give you the real authentic flavour. That's just not possible in books. I mean those touching little stories like you just told us about that water-bottle xylophone just aren't in the books. Do you know what I'd like Mr. Forbush I'd just like to stay up here with you for a while. I really would that would be the greatest thing that ever happened to me but I suppose I'll just have to be content with meeting you and I'll tell everybody back home about what you're doing down here living in this historic place and spending all your time with the penguins like that. I think it's great. I really do."

Forbush was exhausted. At last he could lead them outside and in careful single file across the lake to the rookery. Judge Coxfoot fell over on the ice seven times and had to be picked up by Lieutenant John Smith Cranford Junior and brushed free of snow. Only Evan Jenkins walked with swinging sure steps behind Forbush who, as they approached the penguins thought of the disturbance all these people would cause and began to hate them. He became uncommunicative.

"Gee what a cute little bird. Can I pick it up?" asked Evan Jenkins.

"Yes."

"In my bare hands? I'd just love to feel what they feel like."

"Why not?"

The penguin bit Evan Jenkins so hard that he lost all the skin off his left hand knuckles and Forbush felt his spirits soar when he saw that Evan Jenkins' jacket was covered in bile-green guano.

When David Goldthwaite asked if the skua gulls were friendly too, Forbush told him to walk up the little hill at the north end of the rookery because there was a fine pair of skuas up there and David Goldthwaite did—and lay crouching on the ground with his hands over his head when the skuas screamed and dive-bombed him and beat him on the head with their bony wings.

(They've laid an egg, they must have laid an egg. Go! Go! Go! You beauties.) Forbush cheered mentally while David

Goldthwaite lay on the ground clutching his head and called "Help." Forbush had visions of himself directing vast armies of birds against a hostile empire. He was omnipotent lord of the birds smiting invaders. After a while he rescued the enemy by walking up holding a bamboo marker pole so that the skuas dived at the flag instead of David Goldthwaite who was led trembling from his defeat.

"Sorry about that. They're usually so quiet," Forbush said maliciously and waited impatiently for the others to finish clicking their shutters and dropping flash bulbs, film packs and wet pieces of paper from their polaroid cameras all over the rookery.

It was not until he had led them back over the lake to the hut that he realised Joe Sloberman was not with them. He had vanished. Forbush looked back at the rookery but Joe Sloberman did not seem to be there. He counted the people. One, two, three, four, five, six, seven, eight. Nine?

"I think we've lost somebody."

John Smith Cranford counted everybody. Al Weiser counted everybody. They all made it eight.

"Where's Joe Sloberman?" said Judge Coxfoot and counted everybody. He made it seven and had to count again. They all stared at Forbush accusingly.

"What have you done with Mr. Sloberman?" said the man from *Pravda*.

Forbush excused himself and returned wearily to the rookery. He found Joe Sloberman hiding behind a rock with a penguin on his knee. He was covered in bile-green guano and he was trying to draw a penguin-sized red bathing suit stained with bile-green guano over the penguin's stumpy legs. His lips were bleeding from the cut of a flipper blow and his glasses were askew. His nose was red and dripping.

"What are you doing?" said Forbush.

"I'm putting this bathing suit on this penguin," said Joe Sloberman.

"Why?" said Forbush.

"Because a public relations man in Oceanville wanted me to," said Joe Sloberman.

"*Why?*" said Forbush.

"Because every year in Oceanville we have a big carnival

and one of the things about this carnival is we have a little man in a red bathing suit as a sort of a symbol or something and this man (ow) this public relations man (keep *still* you . . .) this public relations man thought it would be a good thing to have a picture (ow) a picture (oh hell I've got this green stuff all over me) a picture of a little penguin all the way from Antarctica wearing this little red bathing suit to use in the carnival. I mean it would be kind of cute wouldn't it (ow) wouldn't it?"

"*You bloody idiot,*" said Forbush.

"I beg your pardon?" said Joe Sloberman.

"I said you bloody idiot. Put it down. Let it go. For God's sake you're a bloody idiot. Where did you get it? What's happened to its eggs? Oh my God you've killed two more. You've killed them you bloody idiot. How can you be so ignorant? Get out! Get out of here! They're all dying you fool. Dying—for a bloody red bathing suit. You've killed two more!"

"I'm sorry," said Joe Sloberman. He stood up and the guano ran down his trousers and dripped from the red bathing suit in his limp fat hand. The penguin ran and stumbled blindly towards the sea, pecked and beaten in its panic through the colonies.

"Go on. Go back to the hut. They're waiting for you."

"I'm sorry . . . I feel such a fool . . . I mean I really did mean it was great to be here Mr. Forbush . . . now I've gone and spoiled it . . . it was so stupid but I didn't know what to do . . . I'm sorry," said Joe Sloberman.

They left him mail and at least he remembered to post his own pile of letters home. Evan Jenkins had presented him with a clipping of his first story in the *Harrisburg Enquirer.* "I walked round the world in just fifteen seconds and in temperatures ranging from minus 30 to minus 80 degrees F.—at the South Pole!" and "of course living in the Antarctic is pretty easy these days although we are suffering some hardship."

Barbara sent him, copied in her careful writing, a translation of a Mayakovsky poem written, she said, just before his suicide:

"She loves me? She loves me not . . .? I'll cut my hand off, fling aside my severed fingers. They'll scatter on the wind like petals from the wayside flowers, the camomiles that lovers pick to tell their fortunes. . . .

"I swear that I shall never speak with the shameful tongue of common sense.

"Past one o'clock—you must be sleeping. Or perhaps you too. . . .

"The tide is ebbing into sleep. So let us say: 'The fun is over. Now you and I are quits. Why should we chart our wrongs and hurts and grievances? Love's boat has piled on the reef called Commonplace and now breaks up.'

"Past one o'clock—you must be sleeping. The Milky Way spreads like a river through the night upon her huge and silver course.

"Look. How quiet it is. All the earth is silent. Night has embraced the sky with a gift of stars. Now can a man stand, speak, his words echoing through the ages, history and all Creation."

She had written "Don't let it ever be like this for you, Forbush. It's too beautiful, tragic, hopeless. Never be like this."

He felt the strength locked paradoxically in the very tenuousness of their relationship.

It was well past noon and the sky was darkening from the south, the ice turning bitter and grey, the mountain smoke plume blowing hard and straight as Forbush went to sleep.

CHAPTER SEVEN

FORBUSH knew about the blizzard twelve hours before it began. He woke at six o'clock the next morning and felt the air warm on his face when he went outside. He felt that day as if all the wind which was to blow in the next three days was concentrated directly over the Cape and rookery, a monolithic force to which he should pay homage. Somewhere to the west in the centre of the Ross Sea a great cyclone reigned. He basked in the mildness of its calm breathing and knew that it would soon wake to attempt his destruction. He was not sure how it was that he knew the blizzard would blow. The knowledge came from some instinctive awareness of the totality of gathered forces about him. The skuas told him in the way they were aloft riding the air currents swirling round the peaks and gullies of the Cape. The Penguins told him with their huddled calm.

As he went about his morning's work in the rookery he watched the day change and move in preparation. Absorbed in counting or observation he would suddenly become aware of some subtle change in the blizzard's deployment of its gathering forces fearful that he had missed some warning sign, that he was being tricked. He would stand upright and quite still moving only his eyes hoping to catch the blizzard unawares and diminish its power with his knowledge. Always it was too quick. He felt as if he was in a pitch-dark room about which black birds or bats flitted, strange black shapes gliding along the floor and over the walls creating some indiscernible darkening of the darkness, sounds indistinguishable from the scratching of silence of his taut eardrums yet making him intensely aware of their malign presence. He wanted to warn the penguins, speak words of comfort and encouragement to them, inspire them to hold out against the blizzard's strength, to stay at their posts, fight with all their strength, cling to their nests though they died in their desperate and quixotic assertion of life. "Forbush expects that every penguin will do his duty."

He found the penguin that he could pick up. For the first time it showed no sign of alarm when he passed through its colony counting eggs and no longer hissed, pecked and beat his leg with its flippers when he gently lifted it off its eggs with the toe of his mukluk. He crouched down and lifted it up on to his knees, cuddled it against his chest stroking its throat and breast until it stretched its neck forward, swallowed and ruffled its stubbly close-packed feathers. He talked to it in a low voice.

"You must be strong, penguin, you must be strong. Above all don't run away. Let the snow bury you and you'll be safe. Don't worry because I'll come and dig you out. Oh dear you poor wretched penguin . . ."

It was with a sense of horror that he saw the first hen come back from the sea. She was not distinguishable from any of the non-breeding birds arriving at the rookery until he saw the purposeful way in which she climbed the slope from Access Beach and made her way through the colonies directly to her mate and nest.

"Thank God he's there," said Forbush aloud as he watched ten yards away.

The hen was plump and shining beside her scrawny guano-stained mate. A few yards from the nest she gave a loud squawk of recognition and greeting which he answered standing erect and expectant. Together they began their ecstatic mutual display bending over the eggs with twisting, waving necks and bowing to one another with delight. How soon would the eggs hatch? How long would it be before the blind chick, all bulging stomach and disproportionate beak, would begin its long battle with the protecting shell, the steady chipping which would take as long as three days to release it to its first-born day? Forbush waited until the pair changed places on the eggs and the cock bird began the last weary task of laying stones upon the nest before he departed to break his weeks of fast.

He went next to the nest scoop in which the first skua hen had laid her eggs, holding his marker pole high against attack by the screaming pair and almost standing on the mottled brown eggs before he saw them lying in their slight depression. They had been laid with little fuss, for the skua's way was to forage free until the last few hurried hours in which the nest scoop would be cleared before laying with a lack of ceremony characteristic of savage, self-reliant creatures. Forbush wondered why, as the blizzard gathered about him, he could hardly wish their eggs ill.

He knew it would not be the kind of wind which a man loved because he could battle with it in some fair division of odds, the wind with which he struggled on a hilltop while all the earth and trees and grass struggled with him, the wet salt wind of the sea which had to be endured and overcome and yet would leave him with a sense of kinship. This would be a wind that tried to destroy him, that expressed its enmity with every howl and blow, that would be vicious, without restraint or mercy. As the day drew on, the knowledge made him feel thin inside, mean and calloused in his heart.

He kept searching for some positive sign, the declaration of intention from the wind but such chivalrous notice was never given. Late in the afternoon he climbed Flagstaff Hill to the highest point of the Cape itself. He had never felt so confined. The snow-free lava rocks made a carefully prescribed boundary with the snow field on the lower slopes of Erebus beyond the Blue Lake and the sea ice from Backdoor Bay round the Cape to Horseshoe Bay two miles north with its icy cliffs.

"This is where we must fight it out," he thought. "Here we have two square miles of earth or rather rock. The wind will come straight up the Sound, just east or south with nothing to limit its force once it's free of Minna Bluff and the islands. The penguins should manage because they nest on the lee slopes mainly. The skuas are cunning enough to keep below the ridge tops. Why should I worry about them? I don't know. O hell we're all creatures. I'm a creature. At this moment I'm no different from them. I've got my brain and my stereoscopic vision and my long legs and my ingenious hands but they are really much more clever than I because they've done this for a million years. How small I am, smaller than the penguins, less swift than the skuas, ignorant of nature. I've no built-in protective devices to keep me safe in this at all. All I have is an old hut tied down with a few bits of wire rope. It hasn't even got any foundations because the ground is too frozen to take them. It just sits there in its little gully and hopes and endures. Well it will endure with me. And you, you bloody old smoking mountain. Don't you be proud and superior. We've got blood, moving limbs, we've got sight and smell, we'll beat you yet. And when your fires are cold our kind will still be burning."

An eddy of wind from the north whipped his face with cold pain which seemed precise and delicately placed to wound him. He flinched in a hard knot and his nostrils quivered. "I'm a creature. I'm no more than a creature. O God give me clear eyes and strong limbs to fight it."

A billowing cloud of blown snow lay on the northerly slopes of the mountain fifteen miles away yet appearing so close in the clear air that he felt he could reach out and touch it. The sky above him was arched with high cirrus cloud, the mare's tails of windy weather. The western mountains were clearly defined across the Sound and in the south the islands grew and faded with the mirage as cold clear air sank down the mountain glaciers and lay like a liquid sheet across the sea ice, a natural prism at its boundary with the warmer air above it, catching and bending the images of islands, glacier tongue and ice shelves, heaving them skywards into grotesque and bulging reflections of themselves inverted.

He noticed that but for an hour or two at midnight the days were losing their gold now, the spring radiance of the low sun, and that the colours of the day were black, white and blue in much more definite and cold proportion. His "Polar Penguin Producers" sign wavered and shook in an eddy of wind. "It's firmly enough based. It shouldn't blow away." The door of Shackleton's meteorological screen beside the hut began to bang gently and he heard its knocking across the frozen lake. His bamboo aerial mast wavered and was still.

He looked south again, still standing stiffly and with pinched nostrils, alert. The cold air flooding into the Sound was now seeping north about the islands of Erebus Bay, the Erebus Glacier Tongue which turned into a line of white battlements and Cape Evans which turned into a jagged ridge piercing the sea with savage peaks. The ice falls beyond it caught the sun and gleamed so bright that his eyes were burned and the crevasses were so enlarged and deep and dark that the ice formed itself into rows of rending teeth.

He could see the wind coming, hours away. First Minna Bluff simply disappeared. He looked and it was not there. The wind was coming. Minna Bluff seventy miles away was obliterated in a boiling cloud of snow. And then Black Island fifty miles away. The wind was coming and he would not know it until it was there around his feet and growing thicker, creeping round his ankles like an ocean tide, passing him, travelling north, creeping deeper and deeper, moving steadily and with resource and certainty, not hurrying because knowing its own strength it had no need of haste, creeping on above the tops of his mukluks until it fluttered in his baggy windproof trousers, until it licked like cold fire under the tightly-drawn bottom of his anarak.

(Remember on a beach among the sand dunes and hot marram grass you would see small sandstorms and eddies of sand grains in the wind, you would see their smallness and yet they would sting so that you felt they were big and the wind was big to blow and force them. Well, look now, there fifty miles away the snowstorm looks like those small eddies of sand and you cannot feel any of its strength but if you stand here on Flagstaff Hill and look for long enough you will begin to understand the terrible enormous strength of the wind and snow. This would not merely sting me . . . it would annihilate me . . . me, myself, I would be a mere grain and part of the eddy, a small piece of wind upthrust among the lava peaks, up over the smoking mountain which is desolate without trees.)

He could not see Observation Hill, Mount Discovery, Black Island, White Island, the indistinct animal shape of Brown Island. He could not see Castle Rock, Ford Rock. The far slopes of the Erebus Glacier did not exist any more. "It is time to go, to batten down, make ready. I must get snow. I'll have to sit this out. I'll have to make the radio aerial fast. The shutters on the south wall windows. How can I fasten the outer door?"

He saw the wind flow in to Backdoor Bay and then into Arrival Bay almost at his feet where Shackleton had come with the brave and tiny *Nimrod* (the great hunter, a mighty name for such a ship), and heaved with swinging boom and strong tackle all the goods and chattels of his small grey hut on to the shore. Forbush saw the wind enter the bay in little rivulets and streams of drift snow blowing inches high and gently above the surface of the ice so that its blue was streaked with rippling white banners, and standard-bearers of the blizzard's cohorts.

Forbush stood his ground as the blizzard boiled up about his embattled hill until the drift rose about his feet like mist and then began to billow high above him in the first glory of its assault. The sun was still bright. The wind descended on him, slashed him and raked him with a wounding claw, a clean straight shaft of cold which knocked his jaw askew, ripped open his lips and eyelids and pierced the coiled cells of his brain like the fateful arrow which pierced Harold at Hastings when William bid his archers shoot high and kill the Saxons with sharp rain. Forbush felt the impact of each stinging snowgrain, turned and bent his head to feel the drift compact in a mask of ice upon the warmth of his skin. He was blind and deaf, with no touch or smell, and began to run.

This was the beginning. The blizzard had given its first cuff. He ran and stumbled down the hill, across the lake, falling, crawling a moment, knowing only by instinct how to find his home, crushed so soon. Above the wind he glimpsed the smoking mountain and the sun in the south before the drift engulfed him.

When at last he leaned panting and feeling the ice mat of drift snow cracking and peeling from his face, dripping on to his anarak inside the battered outer door of the hut all his efforts to collect snow, fasten his aerial and place the shutters on the windows seemed to have taken place in some totally exhausting dream. He looked at his watch, hardly able to see in the gloom with his smarting eyes.

A whole hour had passed since he fled from the hill, crawled and scraped his way across the inland reaches of the lake, staggered to the windward wall of the hut and heaved the shutters over the windows forcing their wooden clamps into place as if he heaved against the whole weight of the wind which had hardly yet begun. It had taken him a whole hour to fight the wind, to crawl, to cringe under its lash, to struggle and beat it before it had hardly shown its strength, so that he could drag his snow-box from the hut, snatch up his shovel from the door, and almost run, crouching low in the lee of the weathered haybales up the track to the snow-drift, fight to fill the box with snow when almost every shovel load was blown away, great snowblocks twisting and flying like leaves, when his shovel began to dance and bound away across the drifts, plucked from the snow as he tried to compress the blocks in the box to make more room, so that he jumped and leaped, rolled and crawled after it to grab it, almost too late, himself only an inconsequential fibre in the wind, snatching the shovel and lying curled in the snow for minutes clutching the shovel against his chest, fighting to uncurl his limbs and crawl back, to stand erect for sufficient moments to fill the box and drag it, blinded, back to shelter. Even boulders rolled away from his grasp when he lifted them to prop against the cairn which kept his aerial mast aloft. He leaned against the door, blinded and panting, sucking in the still warm air in tearing, moaning gasps before turning with hammer and long nails to fasten the door close against the wind. The snow he could not keep out for, fine as flour, it found its way through every crevice in the doorway to pile sifted in the passage growing steadily with every hiss of the wind.

Forbush dragged the box of snow inside the hut. "This is all I have, all I have to fight it with."

His watch said that it was seven o'clock on the night of 19 December. The world would never be the same again. He stood in the centre of the hut before the cold iron stove and recognised that this was one of the moments in a person's life which marked a change, the end of an era, the beginning of a new, unknown adventure, a mark on the record of his life like a time mark on a chart recorder—the drum of a barometer or subtle instrument for recording sunshine hours, earthquakes, or magnetic fluctuations—from which years later he might read his own history.

The world was changed utterly, its weeks of golden evenings obliterated in the noise, the shrieking, roaring, drumming, beating blizzard that had now gripped the hut shaking it bodily so that he heard nothing but the sound of its struggle with the wind. He stood and shivered, then jumped up and down on the floor. No sound. He clicked his fingers and clapped his hands. No sound. He shouted "Blow, you bastard, blow," he heard his voice faintly while a sort of elation and fearful excitement overcame him. He was shaking with fearfulness and the effort of his fight to lock himself inside. He felt that now he could only stand, quite still in the middle of the floor, and wait, that he could do nothing, that any effort towards self-preservation or the maintenance of life was pointless in the face of this wind. Again he trembled with the sick feeling of being alone, not despairing or weak or cowardly or pitiful but the sick loneliness of exhaustion that churned in his stomach and rose in his throat until he felt choked and cold, bloodless and sweating. "God I'm a victim, I'm nothing but a victim, no weapons, nothing but hope and what's the use of hope?"

The hut shook and thundered under the growing violence of the wind and drift snow hissed against the south wall like a steam jet while Forbush stumbled to the bucket which served as his rubbish tin and knelt on the floor retching, gasping and clutching his hands tight about his chest as every shudder of the hut was echoed by a convulsion of his body until he sank back on his heels, hands over his face, no longer a creature, his heart so slow that he was hardly aware of its beat, his breath cold on his damp palms. All the warmth and colours of his past swam before his eyes, all the tenderness, the longing, the comforts of human kindness, the gold of sunshine and the green of calm trees, femininity and the kinship of men, sleep and the inspiration of music. At last he was calm and weak so that it seemed as though the noise of the wind was the natural background to his existence and he no longer flinched to its blows.

"I suppose it's all something to do with adrenalin," he thought, eyes still closed but knowing he could now open them and face the world. The hut was dark without light from the south wall and because the sky was now overcast and the air thick with drift. He thought of lighting a paraffin lamp but decided it would be safer to conserve fuel even though its yellow glow could have been company.

"I must have food. I'm alone. That's obvious. That needn't worry me. I've known it all along. The symptoms of fear are created by glandular reactions. Food will dissipate them. In any case I have nothing to fear. Even if the hut blows away I'll find some shelter. I could bury myself in my sleeping bag and sleep it out just as well as the penguins. I needn't worry. I've got fuel and water and food and this hut is tied down with three-inch wire ropes. Anyway it's stood for fifty years so it'll stand out this gale. It's only wind after all. Patience, float with the stream of life, of the wind, waver in it like a fish in a fast current, use life, use your environment, understand it and you'll get by, relax in the stream, it won't harm you, you'll ride it, it won't bear you away."

He began to take off his windproof clothing. The hut was not cold, for southerly blizzards were always accompanied by a temperature rise and his heaters could now easily cope with the summer temperatures. He lit the Primus and melted snow to wash and rinse his mouth carefully of the sick taste of fear. He could see nothing through the north windows but drift in the grey light, whirling and dancing in the lee of the hut where it would settle thickly as long as the blizzard lasted. He thought of the penguins and the skuas and tried to see them in his mind, crouching, backs to the wind, as the drift first grew in long windrows to leeward of their hunched bodies until the drift piles themselves created their own lee and the snow sifted into the furrows between them and the crouching birds until the surface of the rookery grew into an undulant white plain broken by the penguin's necks and black shoulders until even these small shapes created their own piles of drift, until the tide of snow surmounted even their upward stretched beaks and the surface became barren and white, smooth and lifeless.

Forbush cooked himself meat-bar stew flavoured with chilli powder from the looted U.S. Army survival rations. It was almost too hot to eat but he sat savouring and sweating, elbows on the teak table which once was a door aboard *Nimrod* (the mighty hunter before the Lord), glancing roofwards and out through the window like a penguin fearful of a skua's menacing flight each time the blizzard's gust gripped his hut.

"I'm capable again," he thought. "I'm competent. I can deal with this. I don't care how long this bloody wind rages. I'll beat it. It can't hurt me. I'll endure. I'm human. I'm alive and this dead wind is only aimless, moving air. I'll win. I'll stay it out. Why was I sick? Ugh! Ah food. I'm a creature. I'll beat it."

He made cocoa so hot and thick with condensed milk that drinking it was a triumph over a stomach used to hard dehydrated food. It made him feel sick again but this time he jumped up and danced on the floor, grabbed a box on which he stood until he could reach the rafters and performed seventeen chin-ups, then lay on the floor and achieved twenty-five press-ups.

"I'll beat it. I'll beat it. No bloody blizzard'll get the better of me." The rafters shuddered even as his thin hands gripped them and his calloused fingers strained to hang on, their flesh cut and bruised by the angular beams. He began to feel one with the wind, sympathetic to its struggle and churning torment.

"I don't care, you wind. Blow yourself out. I don't care."

At midnight the hut was quite dark and Forbush did not bother to light his lamp but revelled in the blustery night with a sense of being at home in his childish bed while a southerly storm raged untrammelled across the Canterbury Plains and beat around his first home among the tall and bending trees of Christchurch. Darkness and for the first time in weeks he did not have to haul the hood of his sleeping bag over his eyes. He cuddled deep in the warm eiderdown to perform the act of going to sleep, remembering his childish wonder about the miracle of sleep, oblivion, his eyes opening wide with wonder each time the wind howled loudly, and shivering.

In the morning the world was no different. The drift still hissed against the south wall and the hut still shuddered. In the passageway between the inner and outer doors drift snow had piled until it lay two feet deep against the inner door. There was nowhere to put it but in any case he could not go outside. The snow piled deeper and even seeped through the inner door to frost the floor of the hut itself. During the day the wind seemed to settle into a steady rhythm as if the night had brought only the first surges of its flood and now its main stream flowed about the hut drowning in its roaring passage every small domestic noise which could have given him a sense of comfort and safety. It gave no sign of the strength it might develop in the later hours and Forbush slept again that night still wrapped in his wonder at sleep, easy this time because the sound of the wind had become the natural state of his being.

Outside drift snow had covered the surface of the lake and lay deep in the gullies of the Cape. The seal at Access Beach had taken her pup into the sea, now the warmer, safer medium of their existence, and lay with one protective flipper reaching towards her grey child, only her eyes and nostrils above the water, breathing rhythmically and slowly so that her breath sighed each time her nostrils dilated in life with a small sigh that she could not hear above the shrill sighing and hissing of the wind passing over the sea ice and round the stranded growler, the ice hummock and fluting in the reedy crevices of the tide crack.

The skuas lay huddled in the lee of rocks or, if they were the fortunate free birds which had not bred, were soaring and drifting on the wind a hundred miles north over the sea, calm and proficient in their mastery of the storm.

The penguins lay tense athwart their eggs, buried now, sitting out the blizzard with stoic calm, fast to their duty, trapped in their blind assertion of continuing life.

Forbush slept. There was nothing else to do for every living thing about him was sleeping, waiting. He made himself sleep at the time when his recovered limbs were telling him to rise and fight, continue the battle. His sleep was an effort of will, of wilful relaxation in the midst of the tense gale. "Sleep, I must sleep it out. I must sleep. When I wake it will be over. When I wake it will be calm. I must relax, give in, let myself go. I must sleep now and when I wake it will be calm. The world won't be any different. I promise that. The world will be the same. Sleep. O sleep. O peace. O warmth."

How blue and tender was the sunlight through the drawn curtains of his billet room at Wigram Royal New Zealand Air Force station as he tried to sleep after he had left her. Only hours left. In the little cell-like rooms along his corridor the others who would fly south with him that night would soon wake to greet their last day in New Zealand. He could not sleep then and the dawn breeze which made the fresh young silver birch tree beat its sapling branches against his window seemed just as loud with all its promise of life and fruitfulness as this bitter blizzard wind which rocked even his rough bed in Shackleton's hut. Damn having to come back here. Damn having to go south. Damn having to fill in forms, be on time, be one of a group, crack jokes, be a good fellow, get up for breakfast. Damn having to leave her. Damn the sunlight and the green trim lawns of the air force station. Damn the young birch trees whipping his face as he ran down the footpath at ten o'clock to telephone her. Damn having to go in an air force truck with all the other men who would fly south that night and fill in forms, weigh in baggage at the international airport. Damn the aching in his arms and thighs the longing in his heart as he lay in that blue little room as the sun rose, and knew he would be gone in fourteen hours.

When he had left her, where the red rhododendron blossom was crushed at the gate like spilt blood, he had felt so wounded. His heart had opened to her. He was so vulnerable, quivering as if he had no skin and all his raw flesh was exposed to the stinging newness of the day. He woke in his blue room at ten o'clock because John King next door was playing his guitar, a raw Spanish tune to which he sang with a harsh voice. Perhaps, when he telephoned, she would not want to see him? But she did. She expected him to lunch as soon as all his preparations for the night's travel were complete. He had never felt so shy before.

"I thought you'd have to work today."

"I'm sick."

"Oh . . . I'm sorry . . . do you really want. . . ."

"Idiot."

"Hell. Of course I am."

"This is an important day."

"Why?"

"It'll be the only one of its kind at least."

"I suppose it will. Look, its awfully good of you. . . ."

"I'm just a Good Samaritan really."

"Is that all?"

"What more do you want?"

What was she thinking. Probably she was just being kind. Some women had to be kind. Giving in such a way was part of their lives.

"I can't ask for any more."

"Why not try asking?"

"I'll be gone in ten hours." He looked out of the window and the rhododendron tree looked merely like a tree with pretty flowers which might or might not grow or unfold a little more and would certainly fall and rot and die.

"And what do you think I'll do then?"

"I don't know. I suppose you'll just keep on going. After all, we only met last night."

"I suppose I will." Her voice sounded so desolate so that he shivered as if already he was in contact from the ice, climbing down the steep shaky ladder from the Globemaster on to the sea ice runway at Williams Field with the quick cold searing his nostrils and stinging his eyes. He watched her as she stood in her kitchen slicing tomatoes, cutting the rind from thick bacon rashers, filling the salt shaker, lighting the gas stove. She's so capable. How could I ever match that? She's three, four years older than I am yet she doesn't seem to mind me. She's so self-possessed.

"Will you write to me?" he asked.

"Yes."

"I'll write to you. I suppose you won't get many letters. I don't know how often I'll be able to get mail out. I'll do my best."

"I know you will."

"I might write some funny things."

"Oh?"

"Yes. You sometimes write funny things when you're

down there. You get rather worked up. You ramble on a bit."

"I won't mind. Just write to me when you feel like it."

"Don't you want me to write often?"

"When you feel like it. You might forget when you remember all the things you say you'll remember."

"No I won't forget. But I may write some odd things. You won't mind?"

"No. I won't mind. Just write whatever you feel like. I won't mind."

"All right. I'll just write whatever I feel like." The rhododendron tree wavered in the wind and three blood-red flowers dropped. "Thank you."

She came and stood beside him at the window. He saw the greenness of the spring grass.

"You don't have to thank me."

She was so warm in his arms and her dark hair so soft under his hands. Her eyes were soft and searching as she came close to him. She looked fulfilled the way he had never felt a woman look ever before. Damn. Ten hours. Nine-and-a-half.

"I must get you lunch."

"Yes." He was helpless. All the pain and longing and excitement and apprehension swept over him so that he sat in a chair and buried his face in his arms feeling quite alone until she came back from the kitchen.

"Come on. Before it gets cold." The day was hot and windy with the dry breath of a nor-wester. In the afternoon they went walking.

Forbush grew used to the wind. By the end of the second day he felt convinced it would do him no harm although he recognised that this was a dangerous belief and that at any moment it would crush him. His snow box was empty but all he had to do for water was to fill a pot from the snow which still piled up in the passageway. Lighting the paraffin lamp became a necessity, for the drift on the lee side of the hut was so thick that the windows were coated and light shone only dimly through them. The darkness at first accentuated the dismalness of the wind but he became accustomed even to this no longer caring what happened to his home as long as he could feel secure in a cave with warmth and still air.

"Two days. I must have a celebration," he said and, as if he was performing a priestly rite took down his last four cans of beer from the shelf. After all, if Starshot arrived for Christmas he would surely bring some Christmas cheer although the way the blizzard blew suggested there was little hope of Starshot's coming.

CHAPTER EIGHT

"I LOVE you so much," he wrote. "Can a woman ever provide the answer to a man's confusion? Here I am surrounded by such desolation that it occurs to me to wonder if the natural state of life is despairing chaos. Do you know any more than I? When you read this everything that I am enduring and hearing now will be over. The sun will be shining again and the world will be amelt. For all I know the ice might have blown away outside and the sea might be free. I might hear it crashing on the beach when I wake tomorrow. You see, there is a blizzard. It started the day before yesterday and I do not know how much longer it will go on. My life is suddenly surrounded by the closest boundaries it has ever had. The four walls of this hut. I wonder if thinking of you is any real help yet I do think of you. I wonder if I merely use you as a means of escape and, if I do, does that matter. I wait for some resolution of the forces contained in this chaos outside and feel that when it comes it will bear my whole being away with it.

"I am so sad because I think you have stopped being you inside me. You have become only an ideal which pervades my heart and mind and I do not know what to do with it. I suppose that outside some of the creatures are dying and I can no longer understand what is happening to them. I do not know any more the difference between being and not being because within myself the sense of distinction has gone. If the wind blew me away I think I should not have the strength to fight it—or rather the belief. It hasn't really extended me. I just sit here and wait. I'm safe and do not know what I would do if I was not safe and burdened with the decision of preserving my own life. How can I distinguish my own life from the whole of life? Can you be any help? You won't read this for weeks and yet I write as if you will answer me in hours or at least tomorrow. Perhaps my love is idolatrous and I do not know you at all.

"I am drinking my last can of beer but I am not concerned because Alex Fisher the radio operator told me to-night that Starshot is coming for Christmas and Starshot will bring beer. I can trust him. What else can I trust? In any case I am not worried because I have a secret kept even from myself these last eight weeks. I have half a bottle of whisky which I found at the bottom of the stores locker when I arrived here and I don't care if the whole world blows away.

"Can you feel life in yourself? Can you feel your gonads swell, your eggs shed as the rhythm of your life progresses. Do you know any more about life than I do simply because of your sex? Do you know it all by instinct when I must spend these bitter months trying to gain some slight, in-ferior insight, the truth of which I can never really feel? Perhaps a man can never know because his body so con-stantly betrays him into making the creative act and when that is over life demands no further thought from him.

"Damn you. I wish so much I'd never known you. I told you I'd go on the rack for it. And yet it's not the mere sens-ual memory that plagues me. It's the feeling that I was so close to the secret, to knowing the difference. Is love, as the wise people have said, 'the little death'—just as meaningful and meaningless a death as death itself? I cannot describe for you the confusion in which I write inside myself and out-side. The world's aflame and burning with wind.

"I'm so far apart from you now and yet so much closer.

"Why did you send the poem? What's the point of that? What does it matter? Our minds are such victims of our bodies' continuing life.

"Now I'm shouting into the void, the great void of the wind and the ice. There's nowhere else in the world you can do it. You can sit here all alone in this miserable hut in the middle of a miserable blizzard that's busy killing things, and howl into the void. The echoes go round and round and nothing happens. You just sit here and howl 'Why?'. No-body hears you, no voice replies faint with distance. But I must have an answer. Answer me for God's sake. What's going on? There aren't even stars to howl at and the sun's been blown right away. Everything is white. I can't see any-thing out the window except white, white, white. It's so sterile and white. Come to me with your colours and warmth. Who am I writing to? Is it you? Would you answer or are you merely part of the void, a projection of emptiness in the emptiness of space creating only another confusing echo?

"I wish I could go mad and foam at the mouth or something."

On the morning of the third day Forbush lay in his bunk looking at the Penguin Major Polyphonic Music Machine or rather at the sad collection of bottles which was its beginning. Groping under his bunk he found Alphonse in his fragile box and pressed his windy stomach, hardly able to hear him squeak over the hiss of drift and the rumble of the wind.

"I mustn't. No. I mustn't," he thought. Then he got out of bed and stood beside the bottles and pieces of timber which still lay where he had left them more than a week before. "I mustn't," he said as he lit the Primus and filled Shackleton's big rusty pot with snow. "I mustn't, I mustn't," as he dressed in warm woollen clothing and lit his stoves. "I mustn't," as he laid Alphonse on the table and gave his stomach another squeak, as he took his clarinet from its case and blew middle C, a note which was hardly distinguishable from the note of the wind about his door, about the shuttered windows, the straining wires holding down his roof.

"I mustn't," as he picked up an empty mildewed bottle testing its weight to consider whether or not it would give the right tonal warmth upon which to construct the scales of the P.Ma.P.M.M. He would, he thought, and stood quite still for some minutes in the grip of inspiration, hearing all the demonic elements shrieking round him.

He worked quickly, first cleaning all his array of bottles removing the venerable 1906 labels. Heinz had fifty-seven varieties even then, he saw with surprise but feeling hardly a shadow of guilt as the faded papers peeled from the pale green glass.

Professor T. Edgeworth David's test-tubes were the most difficult. Forbush was not quite sure that they would not vindictively blow up in his face with all the explosive force of scientific passion which led Professor David, a young man then, to plod before his sledge all the way to the South Magnetic Pole and back in 1908 when Shackleton was enduring the bitter Plateau near the Pole itself.

Wreathed in steam from his bubbling pot Forbush felt that the shades of all those men past were about him and surely blessing him in his musical endeavours.

Out of the timber from Shackleton's horse-stalls he built a pedestal on a stand and then a cleverly constructed rack on top of the pedestal to hold the bottles ranging from test-tubes to a half-gallon flagon which had once contained formalin. He hardly heard the hammer blows for the wind seemed to be rising.

To the bottom of the pedestal he attached Alphonse in a handy position for right foot squeaking and then considered the nature of the instrument to which his left foot should respond. A drum was preferable to cymbals yet a drum gave a mere single note and some sort of continuous background would be needed to complete the polyphony of the machine. Deep thought was necessary here and Forbush reached for the whisky bottle, peering outside as he poured himself a drink and noticing that the drift still seemed very thick even though he had expected that by now most local loose snow would have been blown away and the atmosphere become fairly clear in spite of the wind.

The great creative thought came as the whisky bottle was nearly empty. "If I make a foot pedal I could have both a banging drum and a continuous scraping brush. Ah."

The foot pedal needed a spring or some rubber, no, it wouldn't need either if he fastened it to his foot so that he could lift it as well as push it down. The brush could be manufactured from some more of Shackleton's toaster and attached to an arm which moved with the foot pedal so that the brush rubbed on an aluminium plate nailed to a crossbar attached to the pedestal. The drum was more difficult. The drumstick had to be hinged to the foot pedal with wire and then attached in a swivelling joint to another crossbar so that its long end and head (made of a frozen potato Forbush found in the corner under the table) could beat on a square drum skilfully fashioned from a penguin skin which had frozen when still wet from the penguin and could be thawed over Shackleton's steaming pot, then carefully sewn on to a wooden framework like a frame for noughts and crosses, stretched and then dried in front of the heaters. It was not very big or very resonant but Forbush, filled with triumph, attached it to a ration box re-modelled to fit and sealed the cracks with candlegrease. It worked. The drum was suspended by meteorological balloon cord from the bottom of the xylophone. "I'm a genius. Tumteetum. *Ai ai ai!*"

He could not decide whether it would be best to suspend his clarinet from a sort of gallows extending above the P.Ma.P.M.M. or clamp it in a canvas and wooden harness over his shoulders. Aesthetically, he concluded it would be best to attach it to the machine suspended over the bottles so that he could pass his xylophone mallet up and down the bottles without hitting it. It looked very beautiful. On top of the clarinet support, like a grotesque figurehead on an antique ship, the P.Ma.P.M.M. was blessed with the plaster figurine of the Venus of Willendorf, her neolithic brow frowning in disapproval at such a musical monstrosity and her gravid belly ready to heave with derisive laughter.

Using Shackleton's white enamel pitcher Forbush now proceeded to fill his xylophone bottles with water to achieve a fine tuning by beating them with the handle of a wooden-handled screwdriver. Including semitones his arm could not stretch more than two octaves but this seemed sufficient. He tried *Three Blind Mice*, and failed miserably, to be overwhelmed with the knowledge that the P.MaP.M.M was indeed a sophisticated instrument that would take considerable co-ordination to master. He had also to face up to the fact that to play the clarinet with one hand was extremely difficult. There was so much noice he could hardly hear a note so that it was not difficult to decide he had done a good day's work in the service of the Muse and lie down on his bunk to gaze admiringly at the machine while he boiled water for coffee.

"I'll have to put it on wheels. It's too heavy to shift easily without them. Aha, wait till Starshot sees this. I'll deafen him." Forbush smiled to himself enchanted with his work and the south-west window blew in.

Instinctively he lunged for the Primus and caught it just as it began to topple with the incredible blast of air which filled the hut like a shellburst so that his eardrums ached with the ramming increase in pressure. In an instant the hut was filled with drift snow almost as fine and thick as smoke.

"The shutter—what's happened to the bloody shutter," Forbush thought as he rolled on to the floor, the extinguished Primus still in his hands. "I've saved that—the stoves, the stoves." He flung himself over the floor half rolling, half crouching to turn them off. "Safe, no fire, no fire. I can't get out. The door's blocked."

He lay on the floor while the snow settled finely on his body and the noise of the blizzard crushed down on him increased by the wild flapping on his canvas curtain, the crash of bottles and tins from the shelves and the creaking and groaning of every timber of the hut. It seemed to Forbush as if the whole building had suddenly become alive, no longer the stoic, solid, safe bulk of a home but a living organ which pulsed with the blizzard and heaved great breaths as its walls and roof met the pressure of the wind.

"What's happened? What's happened?" Forbush spoke aloud but heard the sound only in his inner ear. "I must think carefully. I must think, think, think." He was beating his clenched fists on the floor and rubbing his cheek against the cold boards. "I can't get out. But I can get out through the window. I'm covered in snow. My hand's burnt. I hit my head on the edge of the table. It's bleeding because I can see blood on the snow. On the floor."

The roof gave a sudden heave which Forbush felt in his eardrums but could not see. The noise it made was a terrible dry creaking groan which shuddered even in the floor.

"I'm cold. I'm getting cold. Perhaps I'm going to die like the penguins. I don't care. I don't care about Barbara, about anything, even about the machine. I suppose my clarinet's full of snow. I don't care. I don't care."

He began to move on the floor groping on his stomach, to stretch clutching hands under his bunk until he found his mukluks which he held tight in his left hand. He squirmed on his stomach under the table and round until he reached the ration box wall at the head of his bunk and could stand up, eyes tightly closed, groping upwards and along the curtain wire to find his mukluk linings still hanging where he had left them to dry. The drift was clotting on his eyelashes sticking them together when a gust lifted the curtain and he was surrounded by freezing wind. But he pulled on his mukluks and then his windproof trousers and his anarak and his polar cap and snow goggles which immediately became coated with drift and fogged with the slight warmth of his face so that he had to tear them off.

"Damn. I don't care. I don't care. Damn. Damn you wind. Damn you bastard wind. Damn you. Damn. I don't care."

He lurched towards the shelves at the back of his alcove and sprawled over the table again but found his hammer and a handful of nails which he put in his big anarak pocket. Then he found his climbing rope and ice-axe under the table. He tied the rope around his waist, tied the other end to the low beam above the inner door and with his knife ripped a great jagged square out of his canvas curtain.

The knife seemed blunt and the canvas so tough that it skinned his fingers. "Damn you, damn you, curtain. Damn you, canvas, you'll fill with wind again, the *Nimrod* was never like this you bloody curtain. What can I seal that window with? I can't do it from inside, I can't. I'll have to go out. Wood, I need wood, I need boards. Shackleton's table, he's got a table in there, a table. I'll have to take it."

He lurched across the hut now leaning against the full force of the wind through the gaping window yet unable to see where it was except for the ragged light shape of it. For a few moments in Shackleton's cubicle the air was still and it was quite dark yet the noise of the wind and the heaving walls and roof of the hut made the blizzard even more terrifying. He ripped the boards off the rough table top and staggered back to his alcove for a length of rope. He tied them up and made the free end fast to the beam above the door.

"I'm thinking all right. I don't care. I'm all right. I'll beat you."

He crouched, dragging the timbers, and moved slowly towards the dull light of the window keeping below the full force of the wind until he reached the wall and with a quick heave could push the timber through. He heard it bang against the wall by his head as the wind caught it and pinned it taut against its restraining rope. He crawled through the snow back across the floor for the piece of canvas which he had stuffed in the corner under the table. It was gone. He turned cursing to the curtain again and jumped to smother it for now it flapped wildly, while he slashed another square with his knife and wrapped it round his waist tucked into his climbing rope.

"Now it's me, now I've got to get out. I'm too late, I'm sure I'm too late, I don't care. Barbara. Damn I don't care. Gloves, woolly mitts, windproof gloves, where are they. Trousers. Hip pocket. Damn I can't get them. Ah. My fingers my poor bloody fingers."

The window was easy. He merely gripped his ice axe in both hands, took a stumbling run at it and dived through. The wind stopped him halfway so that he fell downwards dragging the bottom of his anarak and the right leg of his windproof trousers over the jagged glass at the bottom of the frame and ripping them from his waist to his mukluk top so that he lay in the hard-packed snow pressed against the wall and straddling the piles of Shackleton's tinned stores down among which he jammed his axe. The wind cut in against his groin, chilling his leg and knee as if it burned him.

Thoughtless now (afterwards he could not remember a single thought, a single action first formulated in words and then carried out), Forbush heaved himself struggling as if he was glued to the side of the hut, sightless and deaf, his rib cage bruised and crushed against the wall, until his clumsy hands found the straining pile of timber he had thrown out.

Somehow he worked his body over until he covered it, pressing it between himself and the wall so that he could untie the lashing to knot it up again round the remaining boards, which he could then let go as he clutched one and urged his pained body to the edge of the window. In this way, slowly, so very slowly and with infinite effort on each occasion, he was able to nail the boards in place with fingers that bruised and grew more bruised and bleeding until he felt them no longer, remembering at the last to drag his climbing rope free to its full length.

Then, under the slight protection of his sagging body he was able to unroll the canvas from his waist, shedding one set of gloves as he did so because he could not hold on to the stiff hard cloth unless with bare fingers and beginning to feel the ultimate pain in his hands as the raw flesh froze on his finger-ends and skinned knuckles until he could feel the ragged frozen flesh scratching on the cloth, which had to be, had to be (I don't care), had to be nailed neatly and carefully so that the wind would stick it there and not blow it away, nailed over the boards which covered the shattered window. It was.

Forbush lay in the snow, hands stuffed into his armpits, curled into a tight ball, breathing so hard that he knew he could not breathe very much longer and that his limbs would be torn to shreds and shattered by the wind just as the window had been. Then he remembered (God I still remembered) his ice-axe and grovelled for it in the snow, his knees still hunched close to his chest and his eyes pressed tight against his left arm the hand of which was pressed tightly, hurting him, into his right armpit while he clutched at handfuls of snow, searching among the burning cold tins of Shackleton's oatmeal and Irish stew until he found his ice-axe and was able to draw it slowly in towards his chest, burning his right cheek with its cold adze.

He crawled and staggered to the lee of the hut, past the weathered sledge that still stood firmly wedged in the corner, past the door now so stoutly barred against him ("I've locked myself out. Oh God I've locked myself out. I don't care, you bastard, I don't care. I've locked myself out"), past the tiny storeroom on the north-west corner and the notice which said he could not smoke because this was a historic monument, past the motor garage, dragging himself over the lavatory seat buried in the drift snow, and the motor-car wheel and the dog-kennel until he could lean half standing against the yellowed, wind-scoured haybales on the lee wall. His rope was too short. It must have caught on some obstruction and he could not reach the window. He could not find his knife. Where is my knife, my knife, I've had you since I was thirteen years old when I bought you all with my own money and never lost you, where are you, I can't get this knot, where is, where is, oh where is my knife, not now, God, not now, I don't believe in God, not now damn you, my knife, oh it's here, in my hand O hang on while I cut it and don't lose the knife, put it away, O hang on, dig your fingers in, there on the other side of the bale, against the wall, put it away safe, now hang on, crawl, use your axe, dig it in, use the pick in the bales, and hang on, now go past the window, go a little further, a little further, now kick the window, kick it, kick it in, it won't hurt, *aaaah*, now hang on and use the pick of your axe, don't worry about your head, your hat's still on, don't worry, now fall, fall in.

Forbush lay under the upturned table amid the ruins of the P.Ma.P.M.M.'s water-bottle xylophone staring at the drift snow which slowly drifted and billowed through the lee window and listening to the hiss of the wind through the south-west window and the slight hiss of the drift snow. He saw the snow slowly sifting through the tiny cracks which were all he had left of the hole in the south-west window, piling like flour from a floursifter, like flour piling up in the mixing bowl when he used to sift the flour for his mother when he was very young and it was baking day. The blizzard was almost over.

Forbush woke with the pain in his hands and in his knee. The sun was quite shining and the world was still. His sleeping bag was covered with drift snow and it lay in his beard and tickled his nose. The broken north window was draughty so he got up and tacked some cardboard from his empty beer cartons over it. Then he dressed his fingers and the swelling frostbite blister on his knee with sterile bandages and went to sleep again.

At eight o'clock in the morning, Forbush, that indomitable musician, was heard calling Scott Base when Alex Fisher the radio operator tuned his receiver for the emergency listening watch for field parties. Had Starshot left, Forbush was heard to ask in a hoarse and excited voice. No. Starshot was just putting on his anarak to go outside and tow his loaded sledge by tractor to the dog lines where he would harness up his team.

"Well tell him to bring bottles. Bottles. No B for Baker bottles. Got that? Over."

"Roger: I've got bottles. What sort of bottles? Why do you want bottles anyway?"

"I want bottles Alex. I want about three dozen bottles of assorted sizes. And whisky glasses. Tell Star to flog about three of those good whisky glasses from the galley. Glasses. Over."

"All right Dick. All right. You want Star to bring up three dozen assorted bottles and three whisky glasses. Are you all right? Are you all right? Over." ·

"Yes ZLQ I'm all right. I'm all right. Have you anything for me?"

"How did you get on in the blow Dick? Any damage up there?"

"No Alex. Nothing to speak of. Tell Star not to forget the beer. Beer Alex."

"Righto Dick, I'll tell him. We were pretty worried about you up there. We got a peak gust of ninety-five knots here and they were well over the hundred at the airstrip. You must've really bought it up there. Are you all right? Over."

"Yes. I'm all right. Tell Star to bring up half a dozen surgical bandages and some burn dressings will you Alex? It wasn't too bad up here. Not too bad. Pretty boring stuck in here for three days. I've nothing further for you, Alex. This is ZLYR Cape Royds signing off with ZLQ Scott Base. Over and out."

"Are you all right, Dick? Are you all right? ZLYR. ZLYR. Where the hell are you? Fool."

Alex Fisher told the Leader and the Leader said Forbush would be all right. "He's a tough man, Forbush. He's always been a bit mad."

Starshot loaded up his sledge with bottles and beer and surgical bandages. "Are you ready boys," he said and the dogs leapt up in their traces. "*Huit* now, *huit* now boys," and the sledge sped away. Forbush went back to bed.

The pain in his hands woke him again in the afternoon.

There was not much he could do about it because morphine was too dangerous to use with freezing injuries. If he lost the feeling in a wound he would not be able to tell if it froze again. He took four Codeine tablets and sat up in his sleeping bag to light the Primus for cocoa, his head throbbing and his body feeling as if it was afloat in a cold sea. He could not light the heating stoves, for the warmth would melt the drift snow which lay thickly upon every part of the hut, and coat everything with ice when he turned the stoves off. The hut was a wreck.

Tins and bottles from the east and south walls had been sucked on to the floor and some were smashed. King Edward VII and Queen Alexandra's picture lay face down on the floor amid shattered glass. Its frame was split. Several cubic yards of drift snow lay under the broken window and about the door. It was very cold and the snow melted on Forbush's good hand until his fingers were red and chilled. His books and papers were scattered all round the hut, some papers even sticking grotesquely to the chimney over Shackleton's stove. The food in his open ration boxes was covered with snow. It was in his sugar, his potato powder, his cocoa, his split peas and dried vegetables.

"When did I turn the table up the right way? I'm blowed if I remember."

He leaned on the table, his wounded hand extended to the warmth of the Primus. His fingers throbbed and there were sharp pains under each nail. His knee was no longer so painful for it was a simple frostbite blister and swelling. "I suppose I'm lucky."

It was cold, very cold to Forbush. He climbed stiffly from his sleeping bag feeling every bruise on his body, glad that it was too cold to undress and inspect them and rummaged in the snow for his eiderdown jacket, trousers and slippers. In these he felt hardly warmer but at least protected and not losing any more heat. "Heat is energy. Energy is food. I must have hot food."

Clumsily he broke a meat-bar into the pressure cooker, and poured vegetables and potatoes in with it. He made cocoa and then thick soup to eat with butter-laden sledging biscuits feeling the pain recede with every mouthful. In twenty minutes he was eating his steaming stew and sweating in his downclothing. "It's like magic. Food. It's like magic. I feel great." Then he almost fainted and lay down again. "The P.Ma.P.M.M. Damn I broke the bottles. I'll have to start again."

When he woke he felt stronger, got up and dressed, began to dig the snow out of the passageway between the doors. The sun was bright outside. First he had to rake the snow back into the hut with his small shovel held carefully in his good right hand. Then he could open the front door. The air outside was quite still. It was warm. Warm. O warm. No day was ever greeted with such joy, the calm and dreaming world so loved and beckoning. "Where have you gone, blizzard? You leave me as if I had never known your embrace."

Slowly he began to walk, stiff and hobbling, over the snowdrifts towards the lake. The snow was packed and scoured so hard that his feet hardly sank in. He walked with a shining face out across the lake towards the rookery, which was silent. On the slopes where there was least shelter from the wind the penguins sat beside little pyramids of drift which had formed on their lee side. He could not see one stiff dead bird. The lee slopes where the snow lay thick were peppered with small dark holes from which sleek black heads and curious beaks occasionally emerged to inspect the sky. No wind. No clouds. It was over.

He walked on and up over the rookery snowslopes pausing to raise his "Polar Penguin Producers" sign, scrape the icy snow off its face and set it firmly again in its cairn of stones. The birds made no sound. Even the skuas were silent, resting from flight against the warm rocks of their ridge tops. In the whole rookery there were three dead penguins.

The snow was melting quickly about dark stones which absorbed the sun's heat and about the penguins' dark heads and backs. In another day most of them would be free of snow. Forbush stopped by the penguin which he could pick up and with his free hand scraped away the snow around it. The two eggs were tucked firmly between its thighs and still warm. It blinked and turned away its head when Forbush raised its breast above the eggs. "I told you. I told you so. You're safe." But they didn't need me to tell them. They knew so well. We've come through.

The air was still and the sun high over the western mountains, bright on the ice falls of the mountain which hardly smoked at all, shining about the islands of the Sound. The ice was blue and fast to the north as far as he could see. He became aware of a sound, a sound of water like a mountain stream trickling among stones, through moss and under shady tussocks, and knew that for the penguins the true trial of the blizzard was just beginning. As the snow thawed the rookery would be flooded. Now he could hear the flood begin with the first seeping trickle of the thaw running amongst the nest stones of the penguins, down the gutters and gullies of the rookery into the lake, all unseen under the clean blizzard snowdrifts.

CHAPTER NINE

STARSHOT was coming. As Forbush stood in the rookery listening to the menace of the flood Starshot was running with his dogs across the sea ice near the end of the Erebus Glacier Tongue. He was running because there were seals about and pupping beside the big pressure crack which ran from the end of the Glacier Tongue to Inaccessible Island, and the network of smaller cracks which radiated from it. He was cursing and out of breath because the dogs, straining, with their tongues hanging out, kept running towards the seals instead of on a steady course for Cape Evans. Starshot had to kick off his skis, first the one nearest the side of the sledge, deftly thrusting it forward so that it ran with the running sledge while he rested his inside foot on the footrest under the sledgehandles, while he bent down and lifted the ski up on to the sledge and thrust it between the lashings of his load, and then the outside ski when he kicked his foot free of its loose binding, and riding the sledge with one leg and a hand clinging, picked it up to place it with its pair on the sledge. "*Owk* Butch, you silly bastard. *Owk Owk*," he shouted in the midst of these acrobatics, commanding a swing to the right from the big white lead dog with the brown patch on his left ear.

Butch looked back at Starshot over his left shoulder with his tongue hanging out requesting confirmation that he was doing an excellent job. "*Owk. Owk* Butch. I'll fix you, you thick-headed, mangy fool of a dog." Starshot sprinted, clumsy in his mukluks, wide from the sledge to the head of the nine-dog trace and heaved a lump of hard-packed snow which caught Butch on the left eye and turned him effectively. "*Huit* now, *huit* now boys. *Huit* Peabrain, *Huit* Peanuts. *Imiak*, Singarnet, Selutok, *huit* now."

As Forbush wandered back from the hill thinking of the menace of the flood and the implacably firm sea ice Starshot ran to the head of his team, way out front so that his shacking trot was just a little faster than the dogs' four or five miles an hour and led Butch towards a low spot in the upthrust pressure ice along the big crack between the Glacier Tongue and Inaccessible Island, jumped it and ran on "*Huit* now, *huit* now boys," so that the dogs leapt the crack without a pause and bounded bright-eyed and eager after him, so that the bucking sledge hit the crack, its stiff-sprung hickory taking the force of the blow so that its runners bent and drummed on the hard ice and its load was heaved up and down, crash, across the crack and safe on the other side while the basking seals rolled on their backs and raised their short necks and sluggish heads, hissing in alarm.

Forbush plodded back across the snow lake feeling the menace of the flood and watched the skuas which lolled about their rocky roosts like unrepentant criminals safe and resting, pirates languid under the palm trees of their desert islands dreaming of plunder, as Starshot led his team free of a few hundred yards of hummocky ice and fell back to jump on the sledge, riding the runners while leaning over it so that the load supported his heaving chest, and then clambering up to sit astride it now that the course was free without the distraction of seals. The ice was bare, blue, slick with the sun and fast for sledging. The runners drummed with a sound like no other sound but the glorious free running sing of a dog sledge and the timbers of the sledge flexed and gave against their rawhide lashings like the timbers of a Viking ship in a seaway. "Let them pull for a while. It's an easy day, sea ice all the way and that's easy sledging. The ice is good and bare. *Huit* now. What the hell does Dick want bottles for?"

As Starshot drove his dogs into the shelter of Cape Evans and stopped the sledge using the brake and calling "*Aaaah* boys, *aaaah*" in a soft voice of descending tone, Forbush sat on his bunk and dressed his hand and knee, too tired to brush any more snow from the hut than that which cleared his own untidy corner and waiting, anxious, for his soup and meat-bar stew.

Portly, short-sighted Starshot was feeding frozen one-pound blocks of pemmican to his dogs, all dancing and howling at the end of their chains heaving against the anchored span wire which held them in a line, while Forbush slept again, his mind floating in a cold sea and his Codeine-drugged body flaccid and at rest.

Starshot, the low sun burnishing his curly golden beard and glinting on his spectacles, pitched his doubled-walled polar tent, carefully poking two holes in the snow with the haft of his ice-axe in which to anchor the back two of the four bamboo poles which, when extended, kept the green canvas stretched tight in a pyramid, and then opening the tent like a fan, spreading the skirts wide to pile anchoring snow blocks on them, staking out the guy ropes. He hummed a song out of tune ("Humm humm I'm singing out of tune") and dug snow blocks to place at the entrance of his tent between the inner and outer walls for water, dug a hole on the other side of the entrance for refuse, heaved his air-bed, sleeping bag roll, kitchen box and pack of personal belongings inside, dumped his ration box at the door and crawled into his beautiful, permanent, unblowndownable green and comforting home.

"Humm humm, that's better. Shut up! There's too much noise out there," for the dogs were yelping and rattling their chains. They whimpered and were quiet. "Humm humm, well I'm blowed."

Starshot made his soup and cooked a large thick lump of steak which the Scott Base cook had given him. Forbush talked softly in his troubled sleep and dreamed he stood on an ice-floe with three jet-black penguins which were terrified of three killer whales which slowly swam round and round, sighing heavily with each emission of their foul, steamy breath, about the ice-floe which melted quite rapidly inwards from its crinkled edge.

"Ravens!" said Forbush and sat up in bed. For the first time he noticed that his head ached from the bump he gave it when he dived for the Primus after the south-west window blew in. He sighed and went to sleep again while Starshot snuffled the detritus of a rich dinner from his beard, slurped his coffee from a big white mug, savouring the rum he had slopped into it, lit his pipe and snuggled into his sleeping bag to enjoy reading a three-year-old issue of the *Saturday Evening Post* which the pemmican makers had packed into the dog pemmican tin. Nobody ever knew why the dog pemmican packers did this but they did and it was one of the more enjoyable mysteries of sledging. He had one day found a battered copy of a nudist magazine which gave him disturbing dreams even though the women were fat and ugly. He was prone to disturbing dreams.

He rose at seven o'clock, rubbed the sleep from his eyes with his dirty fingers, lit his pipe, ate two plates of porridge and half a pound of thick bacon rashers and drank three cups of tea, packed his belongings, struck his tent ("Humm humm, *aaaah* boys, *aaaah*," for Butch and Peabrain were snarling in a fighting mood and this long-drawn, low sound made them quiet), loaded his sledge, hitched up the leaping dogs and was away by nine o'clock, riding the footrests at the back of the sledge and shouting to the dogs with joy over the first wild quarter-mile dash.

At two o'clock in the afternoon Forbush, who had risen late and was performing his first egg count for almost a week heard them coming with Starshot yelling the high rippling call to go left, "*Rrrrrrrruck*" and swearing at Butch only three hundred yards from Arrival Bay. It was Christmas Eve and there were ten penguin chicks with soft blue feet in the rookery.

For some reason Forbush did not go down to greet his friend or offer to help Star span out his dogs, feed them and carry his gear up from the bay.

Forbush sat in the rookery, squatting in a little suntrap among the rocks beside Colony 9 and thinking about the penguins and the skua gulls and seals and how far out the ice was. Not so very far now, he knew, only twenty to thirty miles. The skuas made their fishing flights in a much shorter time and it was certain that the blizzard broke up much of the southern Ross Sea ice. The sea would come soon.

The rookery was alive again. Already most of the snow drifts had disappeared from around the nests and though each bird still sat in a hole in the snow it was free to move, turn its eggs or attend to its chicks. A constant stream of birds was now returning from the sea and the air was filled at times with ecstatic cries of recognition. The return of birds which had lost their eggs early in the incubation period, and were re-discovering their mates to begin again the now pointless task of nest-building, was bringing a steady increase to the rookery population. Forbush wondered why they bothered and could only attribute their behaviour to the ceaseless demand of instinct which ruled their lives.

"Damn. There's a survival reason for everything. Every action has point in terms of survival. Why?" It was obvious that the yearling birds, indentifiable because their throats were white until their adult black throat-feathers appeared at the first moult, would build their untidy nests for practice and the establishment of territorial feelings which would bring them back to the same spot next summer. Forbush made a mental note to test this conclusion by banding a group of yearlings and noting the sites where they made their first nesting attempts. His successors would then be able to draw conclusions about the penguins' establishment of territorial rights.

Faintly he heard Starshot swearing at his dogs but still leaned against his rock, eyes half closed. "At least I'm beginning to feel like a scientist again. Now. Why is it that the skuas don't lay earlier than the penguin? The penguin chicks will be most vulnerable to the skuas in their first two or three weeks and therefore the skuas will get most food. So why don't they hatch their chicks early enough to take advantage of it? But the whole point is that while some skuas get food on the rookery, most of them don't, and those that do stop those that don't from doing. Therefore the skuas' reliance on penguin food must be a very casual one and since it would be screwy for a few skuas to differ from the rest of the species in their breeding behaviour just because they got a bit of free tucker it follows that the association of the skuas with the penguins is fortuitous. The skuas which get the gravy are just first-class opportunists like some other swines I know. In fact—now this is a great thought—in fact the penguins actually benefit from the way in which the skuas prey on them. Because if the skuas weren't real thieves and a handful of them didn't have the whole rookery sewn up then it would be open slather, and there would be hundreds of skuas all beating up the penguins. In fact it's rather like a sort of avian protection racket because the skuas say to the penguins well look here we'll keep off all the other skuas but in return for our services we're going to take the odd egg and chick from you. O.K.? Ai ai ai. I'm a genius. I've made a contribution. Everybody's always assumed that the skuas were dependent on the penguins and that's why they nested close by and nobody's ever seen them fishing at sea. I haven't either but I've seen them regurgitating fish so it follows they must have been fishing. Ha ha! And their breeding cycle isn't even adapted to fit in with the penguins! Well I hate the bloody skuas anyway. I've made a contribution. Get out you butchers."

He leapt up and hurled a stone at two skuas which sat on a rock twenty yards away. Every muscle in his body complained, his head throbbed and the pain was sharp in his fingers. He sat shakily down again. "*Damn.*"

Close by him a small bridge of snow between two nest holes subsided with a mushy sigh into the hollow carved beneath it by the trickling meltwater. The snow melted quite quickly and swelled the trickle to a rivulet. Forbush watched the snowdrift and in a few minutes saw it collapse in half a dozen places. The flood was growing rapidly. He noticed that several penguins nearby were standing anxiously peering from side to side and at their feet, and guessed the flood tide must be rising into their nests. Just as nothing could stop the blizzard the flood had to be endured. A few birds in the wet gullies seemed to be building their nests higher to raise the eggs out of the water. Others stepped from the nests, paused a while, then hopped on to the snow and scuttled towards the sea.

It's all happening so quickly, he thought. It's so sudden and merciless. The skuas pounced to carry off the dripping eggs leaving them after a few vicious pecks if the chick inside was too well formed to be sucked or pulled out. Some birds continued to sit stoically on their nests in spite of the water which rose round their feet and almost covered the eggs. "Bless you," said Forbush. "That's the way. Give it a go."

Starshot was coming, strolling slowly and assured over the

scoria desert towards Pony Lake, looking at the rookery with mild, unblinking eyes. Forbush walked to meet him and stood waiting at the edge of the Lake colony beside his farmyard sign.

"Merry Christmas," said Star.

"Good grief. Is it? I suppose it is. Today or tomorrow? Did you bring the bottles?"

"Yes."

"And the beer?"

"Yes." Starshot took off his pack, sat down on a rock and took out his pipe.

"And the bandages?"

"Yes."

"And the burn dressings?"

"Yes."

"Ah, you beaut. Did you have a good trip?"

"Yes. Not too bad."

"I suppose you're hungry."

"Not too bad. Could do with a brew though."

"How're things at base?"

"Not too bad. Glad to get out for a bit."

"Did you bring any mail?"

"Yes. Bits and pieces."

"How are the dogs?"

"Good. Oh goodoh thanks."

"It's a hell of a season."

"I didn't think it was too bad. The ice is a bit late I suppose."

"Late? It's impossible. The rookery's taken a real bashing."

"Oh? Why's that?"

"They can't get to the sea. They've been starving. It's not so bad now though. I reckon there must be open water at Beaufort Island."

"Yes there is. I'd better not let the dogs get loose had I? They'd soon clean up a few penguins."

"Dogs! Dogs! Look Star if you let any of those dogs loose I'll cut its throat. I'd kill it Star. Dogs. Look you'd better get them out of here. You'd better take them away."

"They're all right, Dick."

"All right! You know what those dogs are like. They're killers, Star. Honestly. You know they are. They just go mad and kill for the sake of it. Oh damn."

"They're all right Dick. Here. Have a smoke. Sit down."

"Yes. Thanks. We've just got a flood on at the moment. Some of them are deserting."

"Humm, humm. That's tough."

"Yes. And the skuas have been really vicious this season Star. Look at them. They've had so far to go to sea. It's been really bad."

"I guessed it wasn't too good, Dick."

"They've been deserting the nests in droves, Star. You know already there's only one third the eggs there were last summer. And there's more going right now. Look. Look at that skua. See it can't even eat that egg. The chick's too big and the skuas can't use their feet—or rather they don't, for some reason or other; I mean they don't use their feet to hang on to things while they use their beaks. So that skua will just leave that egg if it finds something easier. See. I told you. I want to shoot the buggers."

"They're just creatures Dick. I think they're rather fine."

"Yes but—I don't know . . . hell I should know that Star, after all I am a biologist."

"Yes. You're a biologist."

"Oh hell. There's another one. Those low-flying sods have got it all their own way. I can't even hit them with rocks. They're too quick."

"It'll all be the same in a few more seasons, Dick. You know that better than I do. It's just the same. It's the natural order."

"Yes. I don't know."

"Let's go and get a brew."

"Yes. I suppose we'd better. You can't do anything, you see, Star. They just go on and on dying until you'd think there wouldn't be anything more to die anywhere and yet they're still going on dying and it's so desperately hard to live. The smell of them. I know it's only the guano smell but it smells like something else sometimes. It chokes you."

"Yes. It's a powerful smell all right. Come on. Let's get that brew."

"All right. Things are a bit messy up there I'm afraid. I haven't had time to clean up."

"Never mind."

"The window blew in. It sort of wrecked things a bit. I'm sorry."

"In the blizzard, you mean? That was tough. Life's a bit tough, Dick."

"Oh I'm all right."

Starshot did not say anything about the hut. He did not even seem to notice. He simply lit the Primus and made a pot of tea, humming to himself a little out of tune. Forbush did not say much either. He drank his tea and lay down on his bunk. Then Starshot went round the hut and picked up all the tins and bottles which had blown off the shelves, dusted them free of snow and put them back. He stuck some sticking plaster on the framed photograph of King Edward VII and Queen Alexandra and hooked it on to the wall and shook the old reindeer sleeping bags free of snow and brushed the snow off Shackleton's old socks and trousers. He swept the snow off the rafters and window ledges, the stove and the kettles and the remains of Shackleton's toaster. He swept the snow from the floor round the corner where Forbush lived and Forbush did not hear him because he was asleep. He tidied Forbush's books and papers and swept the snow out of the shelves and cupboards. He swept up the remains of the water-bottle xylophone, carefully laying aside one undamaged test-tube previously used by Professor T. Edgeworth David, swept all the snow and rubbish into a pile near the door and then transported it outside in an old cardboard carton. Then he emptied his pack and walked down to his sledge to collect the bottles, glasses, bandages and burn dressings, mail and Christmas cake, cigars and liquor (whisky, port, wine) and trifle frozen in an aluminium foil plate, Christmas pudding in a cloth bag, three plump roast ducklings, a large round yellow cheese, frozen oysters, green peas, beans and strawberries and a very small Christmas tree. He woke Forbush when the meat-bar stew was cooked for dinner.

"Chow down, Dick. Chow down."

"Don't practise your inane Americanisms on me."

"Well stick your dinner then."

"I'm sorry. Oh hell I'm sorry. You've cleaned up too. I'm sorry Star."

"Well eat your soup and shut up."

"Where did you get a Christmas tree?"

"They sent a big one down from Christchurch. I lopped a bit off for us."

"No presents. This is good. I suppose it's just the same as my soup but it tastes different. What have you been doing since I left?"

"Oh just running the dogs and pottering round the ice-shelf doing triangulation for the movement study mainly. Nothing much I suppose. I've been putting in survey stations and strain gauges—you know, we can survey them again next season and find out how much the shelf has moved."

"Mail. I've forgotten my mail."

"Well there it is—right in front of you."

"Ahh. Mail! Hey. Why don't we take a run across the Sound for a couple of days? Why not? Let's get out of this place for a while."

"O.K."

"Boxing Day. We'll go on Boxing Day. Hell. What on earth's my mother got in here? She never could wrap up parcels. A beach towel! Does she think I'm going swimming down here? Do you know the New Zealand Workers' Union has been pursuing me for unpaid union dues for nearly three years. You'd think they'd give up. And somebody's got the idea I'm going on a honeymoon soon. All sorts of literature about snug cottages and secluded beaches. Wouldn't it make you writhe. Well there's not much there. They don't take long to forget about you when you come down here do they? Now. Barbara. You don't know about Barbara do you?"

"No. Something new?"

"Yes. New. I don't know about her myself. I don't think I really understand her. She's a university librarian."

"Not one of those."

"No she's not like that at all. She's very beautiful. I don't know. I've never met anyone like her. She makes me feel.

When I was with her everything seemed significant, out-standing. I only met her the night before we left. I couldn't talk about it on the plane. I was too wrapped up in it."

"A few hours isn't much to go on."

"No. But so much happened. I keep remembering her. Thinking. I don't dare open up this letter. See how it is? She always floors me. She always seems to know so much more than I do. She seems to understand or something. And she has a beautiful skin. All soft and smooth like a baby's."

"Hang on. You'll go under."

"Well it's a kind of a torture. I mean you can't help re-membering what she felt like."

"Don't I know it."

"She doesn't believe in anything. God or anything like that. But she seems to understand something, she's all calm inside as if she knows. It's probably an illusion. I've just probably got to believe in her believing in something or knowing something because I feel as if I don't know any-thing myself. I don't know how many hours I've sat here wondering. O it's good to have company."

"Oh you'll be all right."

"I know. I know. All right. I'll be all right but I can't stop wondering. Excuse me going on about it. It's not guilt or anything. I mean because of her. I mean I'm glad we were together like we were. It was so good. But she made me feel in touch with something I didn't understand. I felt it inside her, it's silly to call it a life force or something. A bit banal . . . But that's what it was. And the same thing's been all around me here. All the time. And it seems to be suffer-ing all the time. I mean it was as if—well, as if Barbara had something inside her that was killing the thing that I felt being alive and growing inside her, flourishing there. That's what it's like here. Something keeps wearing away at me, at life. Just wearing it down like the wind and the drift wearing down the rocks out there. And the ice seems to be holding it all there, you know, as if you were on a rack and your limbs were clamped so that they kept on being toasted over a slow wearing fire, not too hot but just burning con-stantly and wearing you away. I long for the ice to go out.

That seems important . . . I long for it to let go, to let us be free and grow and feed and yet I'm afraid about it because I'll be able to feel when it goes. Feel all raw. But I'm not supposed to be like this, Star. I never was. I mean I went and spent years training and learning how to analyse and look and I rubbished all these emotional things. But here they are . . . I'm sorry . . . And I don't dare open this."

"Want some rum in your coffee?"

"Yes. Yes, that would be good."

"Well you're just lucky because I've still got nearly half a bottle left."

"Oh good for you, Star. You're so eternally phlegmatic. But I know you have bad dreams. I remember you telling me once. Ha ha! We're all the same."

"I don't like thinking about it too much, Dick."

Starshot dressed his hand. It would heal in a day or two, he said. The wounds were not too deep. There would be scars and he might lose one fingernail. The knee blister had dried and there was no danger from it. They would take it easy for Christmas Day and then spend a couple of nights away. They could not risk a longer time because of the ice. The ships were coming, the icebreakers having tough work, very slow, three miles a day or thereabouts still out by Beaufort Island, but they might be in sight from out in the Sound.

Forbush lay in his bunk before listening to Starshot's quick snoring from one of the old bunks in the hut. He held Barbara's letter in his hand feeling its thickness. He found, reading, that it was such an ordinary, normal, comforting letter, full of talk of home, detail, the passing of the season. It described her family and their home in a country town in Canterbury, swimming in the cold green rivers, a willow tree and a hawk, wheat growing in a stony paddock and becoming yellow in the sun, the Christmas shops in Christchurch, the books she had been reading, a play, a concert, her sun tan, her new bathing suit. Nothing about love. Nothing about him. The simple record of her life. He felt nothing except a certain warm pleasure.

She was a very ordinary person. It was a relief that she made no demands on him. She also sent a small parcel. In it were white linen handkerchiefs with his initials and an elegant penguin embroidered in one corner. "I did this," she had written. And nothing else. He felt such an emptiness in his heart and weakness in his limbs. "Why did she send me the poem? 'Don't be like this. It's too tragic'? She's so normal, only a woman. I don't know. O warmth, O peace. I needn't worry. I suppose I'll see her again when I get back. When? When? When?"

For Christmas dinner they had oyster soup, roast duckling and roast chicken stuffed with a special bread, egg powder, mixed herb and kidney stuffing devised by Starshot, strawberries, trifle, Christmas pudding, Christmas cake, cheese, beer, rum and liqueur whisky and cigars. Starshot accomplished this meal because he was sick after the trifle but neither of them minded because they were in a hazy peaceful stupor. Starshot said he was not sick because he was sick but just because he wanted to make a little room. At first he was afraid things would not taste nice after being sick but he had been careful to discard only the top layers of food and not the duckling or special stuffed roast chicken so the taste was not very bad because what he released had not been consumed for long. He had enjoyed the flavour of the strawberries and trifle, however. The cigar made him feel quite sick but he jumped up and ran down to the dogs with their Christmas present—a ski-stick held before each dog in turn so that it could lift its leg, a Christmas luxury in a land without trees or lampposts, he said.

In the evening he helped Forbush do an egg count, holding the book and pencil while Forbush nudged each bird off its nest with his toe, writing down the count, the four strokes crossed out with the fifth ("you'll make such lovely graphs out of these counts"), and getting mixed up in a most unmathematical unsurveyorlike manner (he was squinting a little behind his glasses and kept giggling), in the middle of the larger colonies so they had to go back and start again with Forbush getting extremely bad-tempered. They found thirty-five chicks in twenty-seven nests, all with blue, liquid feet, big heads and bulging stomachs. They saw the skuas take three eggs and batter the shells to draw forth the half-formed chicks, and they threw stones at the skuas laughing every time they missed which was every time they threw a stone. Forbush felt so much better. Company. The ships were coming. The ice was going. There were seventeen seals on the ice about Access Beach. The sun was high and shining. All six skua pairs on rookery territories were safely incubating two eggs and the male birds were courteously and regularly feeding their hens. Hell. Life was good and the sun was high. His hand was healing and it was hardly even cold.

On Boxing Day they got up early, packed their kits and hurried down to the dog lines. They sledged out in a big triangle, first heading south and then in a north-westerly curve until the mountains were clearly seen though they were only in the very middle of the Sound which would take days to cross if they really tried because of the heavy pressure ice on the far side; and then north-east in a circle until they could see the ships. One, two, three, four, five, the fleet in the ice, three icebreakers led by the "mighty G" the U.S.S. *Glacier*, the world's largest icebreaker until the Russians built the mightier nuclear-powered *Lenin*. The *Glacier* followed by two Wind class breakers half her size, followed by the New Zealand Navy's oil tanker followed by a U.S. Military Sea Transport Service cargo ship. The ships were hardly more than dots on the horizon unless the mirage was bright, when they towered up over the ice and each belch of smoke from their stacks billowed up like the smoke of Erebus itself.

They camped out on the ice for two nights. Forbush was stiff with skiing and running and slept deeply. His hand was almost painless now. As he went to sleep each night the dogs performed their "howlo", a series of wavering wolf cries in concert, some high, some low, which each time the little tawny and beautiful bitch, Kari (named by the Greenland Eskimos, meaning Christian), began by raising her head and singing a high, sweet howl. The dogs followed her and sang until the ice was full of soulful music. They then all stopped at once and the silence was utter as Forbush went to sleep. He was still lonely.

"Do you get lonely, Star?" he asked as they stopped on the last day at lunch only five miles from home to drink coffee from a thermos and eat chocolate and rich sledging fruit cake.

"Oh I don't know. It's not too bad. You've always got the dogs. They're always fighting or carrying on or something. You know. You wade in and give the dogs a good beating when they're having a scrap and they all quieten down and get really friendly with you again and you feel pretty good."

"But you have dreams, Star. You told me. You're a thick-skinned sort of fellow aren't you?"

"Yes. I'm thick-skinned Dick. But what's wrong with that? I've got to live my life, haven't I? All right, I have my dreams. So what. I've got dreams. What's that to you, feller . . . Shut up will you, you're going round the twist . . . I'm sorry."

"Yes. Yes. Perhaps I am. Come on. I've got to get back to work."

Are you ready boys, yes, *huit* now, *huit* now boys, yes, and the runners drum on the ice and the sledge pounds, leaping the pressure-cracks, and all the time you hear the scratch, scratch, of the dogs' padding feet, and every time they run through a snowdrift they scoop mouthfuls of snow so that their mouths get cut and bleeding, so that each time they scoop snow they leave streaks of blood upon the shining white snow hillocks and if you look down, and not towards the guiding horizon, the black bulk of the Cape now so near and friendly, you feel you are running and pounding among great rolling mountains and valleys, over them and among them because of the steady swing and rhythm of the sledge. The snow dunes roll and roll so that you feel you are wandering lost and aimless among gigantic rolling and tumbling mountains of snow, you are trapped.

Starshot packed his kit after a night's rest at the hut.

"Don't forget my mail Star."

"No. Don't worry about that Dick."

"O.K. . . . It's been good to have you."

"Good to be here. Christmas back there is always a bit of a drunk. It's messy and nobody bothers to clean up. Can't stand it."

"Well. Look. You've done a lot for me. It's been good. I

feel pretty fit again now. I suppose a blizz like that takes a bit out of you."

"Well take it easy feller. You know. Things'll come right. Don't take the birds too seriously. See you."

"Yes. See you."

He had not even re-built the Penguin Major Polyphonic Music Machine.

CHAPTER TEN

On 3 January there was no snow left on the Cape. At nine o'clock in the morning Forbush came running from the hut, down the gravel slope and across the inland edge of the lake. The ice broke beneath him and he fell up to his thighs in water. He went laughing back to the hut to change his clothes. There was no wind, the temperature was eight degrees above freezing and there were one hundred and eight-seven chicks hatched in the rookery. He walked out to the rookery without windproof clothes and with feet warm in fleecy, soft-soled boots. He sat in his throne on top of the Cape and watched the line of ships which were now pressing slowly south of the Cape only twenty miles from Cape Armitage. Helicopters buzzed like bright red flies back and forth between the ships and McMurdo Station. Sometimes, these days, they flew over the rookery to land behind it on the hill, spill forth half a dozen goggling sailors who would spend half an hour taking pictures of the penguins and Shackleton's hut, and fly away again. Forbush often watched the ships through his binoculars, awed by the power of the icebreakers in their ceaseless attack on the ice. He wished them strength to crush the ice with their massive bows which rode up on it until it cracked under their weight into tumbling blocks which were thrust astern by the plunging current of their propellers. He longed for company when he saw the fleet stopped, the icebreakers parked with their bows resting on the edge of the channel, so that their crews could scramble out on to the ice to light barbecue bonfires, drink canned beer and play football.

But on 3 January the ships were busy and pressing south. Forbush felt himself melting in the warmth of the sun, turning as the leaves of a tree turn towards the sunlight of a new day. He took off all his clothes and lay basking in the warmth and light, his head pillowed on his boots, sad at the whiteness of his skin, the subtle markings of his blizzard bruises which had not quite faded and the grey patches where his skin was dirty. The sun was antiseptic, healing and anaesthetic. He closed his eyes giving himself up to it.

> *The languid afternoon pours*
> *Round my skin, draws in sweet haste*
> *From my heart the first strong course*
> *Of blood so that I lie open*
> *And golden for your taste.*

The sensual memory stirred strongly within him and was followed by a great sadness that his body was pale and bruised and dirty, that he was not golden and glowing with life like a human being, that Antarctica had dried him up, withered him with cold and drought, burned him with ceaseless light so that he had become hard, a half man because he lived on dreams, a grey man because he had surrendered some of his youth, a sad man because he had lost touch with rich and fruitful things which belonged to the warm latitudes which grew trees and women.

"This is no place for a man to live in. I'll be gone soon. Only eight weeks left and I'll be gone. I'll leave it all behind for good. I'll have done my job."

The memory poured over him again until all his flesh tinged with response to it.

"Mere warmth does this, mere warmth from the sun. What sort of person am I now? How far have I come? What will I be like at the end? I merely take off my clothes and my body responds like this to the sun. I can't even control it. My mind doesn't affect its reactions. How did I get like this? How did the place do this to me? I'm no better off than a penguin. They live by the sun, they navigate by it, know their directions by following a meridian of longitude according to their reaction to the sun, the sun's rhythm prepares them for breeding, sends them south, here, sends them north, rules them and directs them. And I, lying here, am powerless in the power of the sun. My great pounding human brain doesn't mean anything at all."

Forbush shivered, not with cold but with some other awareness. He dressed quickly and stood uncertain among the rocks. "There's no point. There's no point in this. Why am I doing it? Why am I here? I must know. I think I know. I can feel the knowing right in front of me but I can't find it." His mind seemed to float from his body, out to the north and over the ice until the savage crowing of a skua beat and echoed on his ears. He shuddered and felt re-integrated, ill at ease.

He watched the skua now standing silent on a nearby rock glancing ceaselessly and quickly about the colony below. It made a sudden lunge into flight, wings wide spread and legs down, wheeled, alighted for an instant to snatch a tiny chick from the nest of a penguin which had been lured away in a pecking match with its neighbour, and returned to its rock. It swallowed the chick whole, head first with stretched and convulsing throat until the legs disappeared still flapping and kicking.

Forbush felt nothing but his continuing faint horror, a resurgence of his ever-present sense of being a victim.

For a week he did nothing but work each day. He forced himself to stop reading and thinking and began each day by making a list of the things he should accomplish. He cut his observation periods to an hour in the morning and an hour in the evening and started a programme of weighing marked chicks, recording the number of feeding times, comparing the weight gains of first and second chicks hatched in each clutch and trying to estimate the survival value of the weight and age advantage gained by the chick which hatched first. A twenty-five-knot wind blew from the north for two days breaking up the sea ice south of Cape Bird so that the sea currents floated it north. Forbush saw open water five miles away. He longed for the sea.

Life in these days seemed so easy. He fell into a new rhythm of thought and activity, full of hope at the coming of the sea, full of pride in the penguins and their now sturdy, well-fed chicks. The whole appearance of the rookery seemed altered. The nest mounds became stained with star patterns of red guano coloured by the krill on which penguins and chicks were feeding. The days were full of the delightful whistling music of the flourishing chicks, a ceaseless sweet sound sung in wavering triplets.

To work with the chicks gave him new faith. Against his

will but knowing it was unavoidable for his study he carried out a series of dissections on newly-hatched chicks to determine the size of the yolk sac which some time before hatching they drew into their stomachs as a reserve food supply should the return of the parent bringing food be delayed. It seemed that each chick was born with enough food to survive three or even four days before its first feeding. He tried a new branding system on the older chicks, consisting of punching holes with a leather punch in the webs of their feet, an activity which amused him and seemed to cause no pain.

When the first skua chicks hatched he even extended his day to enable him to spend two hours a night observing the nest scoops. If skuas were enemies of the penguins they were certainly just as vicious towards each other. In none of the six rookery territory nests in which eggs hatched did the second chick survive more than three days. The firstborn enjoyed a sufficient advantage of weight and strength to gain most of the food brought by both parents in turn and eventually to drive the weaker chick from the nest to be eaten by neighbouring adults. The surviving chicks had to be constantly guarded by one parent. As soon as they had gained sufficient strength to stand and peck, the skua chicks made feeding demands on their parents. Forbush was amazed at their savage tenacity and the intensity of their pleading cries. He had never been so strongly aware of life's demand for death in order to maintain itself. He felt trapped within a cycle so unvarying that the difference between life and death was illusionary, a cycle in which dead things were just as lively as the manifestly alive because each was totally dependent upon the other.

By mid-January the sea was only three miles out but its nearness brought no respite for the penguins and Forbush began again to feel a certain despair. He was almost sick one evening when he was weighing a skua chick after feeding. It regurgitated a mixture of fishy oil and penguin flesh on to his hands. Mindless of its crime the chick nestled in his hands, plump with speckled white down, legs like small sticks scraping his palms, beak already large and cruel, eyes round and bright hard.

He knew it would get worse. The penguin chicks were almost ready to merge from the guard stage of their rearing, during which they stayed on the nest under the protection of one parent, and to form their crèches in which they gathered together gaining a certain safety from numbers while both parents went to sea to catch food to meet their rising demand. Bold from the rigours of the season the skuas would be watchful for the chick which strayed from the protection of the crèche or through malnutrition became too weak to run from an attack.

Towards the end of the guard stage Forbush analysed his population figures. There were five hundred and thirty chicks in the rookery, well under one-third of last season's estimate. Depressed he turned to the P.Ma.P.M.M. and rebuilt the water-bottle xylophone admiring the tone derived from the whisky glasses. He cut his nightly observation of the skua chicks and practised playing it.

Music was little help and he began walking out across the sea ice to inspect the cracks, or north along the shore to see if the sea had come any nearer. The iceberg south of Cape Bird had gone floating north in the Ross Sea currents and the Sound seemed strangely bare and free without it. He found the answer to a problem which had puzzled him for some weeks. Timing the flights of skuas from their nests he found that a standard flight of about an hour and a half was made to the sea for food but there were other inexplicable absences of about half an hour after which no food was offered to the chicks.

He discovered that the skuas were using Coast Lake about three-quarters of a mile north of the penguin rookery as a bathing pond and preening place. At least a hundred were gathered at the now ice-free lake. After several hours' observation on a still and golden evening he deduced that they were coming from rookeries well north and south of the Cape and that non-breeding birds were also roosting there, a pleasant, sheltered spot not far now from the open sea and fishing. He sat on a hillock a hundred feet above the lake and sixty or seventy yards south of it to watch the skuas at their sport and toilet, wheeling and turning in flight across the still water as if playing tag, bathing at the lake edge tossing water over their ruffled feathers or standing on the shore preening themselves with a concentration that to Forbush was full of menace because it suggested the ruthless precision of their unexcelled flight. He felt like an espionage agent coming with surprise upon the hidden headquarters of an enemy guerrilla force and lay among the rocks with his binoculars, carefully noting the flight patterns of newly arriving birds, their bathing behaviour and their preening routine. He felt the sense of power which comes from knowing without being known. Here the enemy rested and prepared for further attacks. Thus armed with knowledge he could plan a campaign.

The ice edge was no more than a mile north of Coast Lake. The deep blue of the sea was like no other sea blue, pure and glowing among the whiteness of the ice. In the unruffled lake the mountains were reflected, even the smoking mountain itself, trapped there in reverse image. He tramped home to supper and letter-writing.

"Dear Barbara—Thank you for your Christmas letter and the handkerchiefs. Even though I'm very short of handkerchiefs I don't dare use this one. Desecration with my dirt. I wonder what you are really like. Your letter helped. I suddenly became aware of other things in you. This will probably be the last letter you will get before I come home. I expect to be flying out about the end of next month—that is only six weeks away—and there won't be much traffic between here and Scott Base between now and then. I'm going all stiff and formal with you. Sorry. I think I've got too isolated. I can't even escape in day-dreams any more. I feel all gnarled. I almost want to hurt you. There can't be any such thing as the love of a good woman. There are fewer penguins growing up this year than ever before for years and years I think. It's the ice and the skuas. Well I'm going to build a catapult. That will fix them. That's my great idea, my contribution. I knew I could do something and that's what it is. I've built a polyphonic music machine which really works (alas I can't bring it home), so surely I can build a giant catapult. That's it, a giant catapult. And bombard the bastards. I've found out where they go, you see. Tonight, just a few hours ago, I discovered where they all go to bathe and preen, hundreds of them. That's where I can get them. I'm too chivalrous. It wouldn't be fair to shoot them here and I haven't got a rifle anyway. The odds would be too much on my side. Well I'm going to build a catapult and get them that way over at Coast Lake. I've had enough. They've had it their own way for too long so now I'm going to interfere. I'll let you know how it goes.

R. J."

He thought, after he had sealed the letter in an envelope that it was not very good so he wrote another one.

"I should see you at the beginning of March. I'll telegraph you when I'm coming. Will that be all right? Hell I've got no idea whether or not you'll want to see me anyway. We're so far apart. Is there anything left? What did you mean by 'it's too tragic'? It gives me a pain in my chest to write and ask you. My stomach is turning over and over. I'm a victim. Will you be there? I suppose you don't really understand. If only there was a word from you. Some greeting. Regards. Dick."

Fortunately Al Weiser dropped by with his helicopter next day and brought him a letter which said she was wondering how he was getting on and if he was well. She was disturbed by his letter during the blizzard. No. She didn't feel her eggs shedding (damn her why can't she take it seriously). She was thinking about taking a short holiday somewhere round about the beginning of March.

He asked Al Weiser to come back the next day with lengths of heavy rubber belting or something like that because he was making a special type of fish trap for a special scientific programme which had to be carried out as soon as there was open water off the Cape and the fish trap could not work properly without a very strong elastic device for shutting its door. Al Weiser believed him.

That night he transported timber from Shackleton's

horsestalls and the runners from an old sledge uncovered by a thawed snowdrift to the hill above Coast Lake where he erected a U-shaped structure three feet high and firmly braced to a six foot length of six-inch-square timber. Carrying it exhausted him but he felt not the slightest bit guilty. The war was just. He wished he could construct a turntable so that the base beam could be swivelled to aim the catapult in any direction but this was obviously beyond his means.

Instead he anchored it on top of a flat lava outcrop aimed directly at the centre of the lake. At the end of the beam opposite the catapult arms he built a winch drum on which he wound a piece of his climbing rope. This would haul back the catapult sling against the tension of the rubber which Al Weiser would bring. The trigger system bothered him and he considered a number of methods involving hooks, clamps, pins or pieces of string which could be cut at the precise moment of firing. Cumbersome though it was a piece of string or, rather, balloon cord was the obvious answer. He made an eye-splice in the end of the winch rope. To this he could attach the cord which would then be fastened to the sling which would be released when the cord was cut to carry a two-pound boulder in a powerful high trajectory clear across the seventy yards to the lake edge into the midst of the opposing army of wheeling, turning, splashing, swimming skua gulls. Then he went home and cut a piece out of one of Shackleton's reindeer sleeping bags to use for the boulder holder at the end of the rubber sling. He felt rather bad about that but it had to be done.

When Al Weiser did not come back for five whole days he became very depressed but eventually the red helicopter flew over the hut with its door open and the crewman dropped a parcel for Forbush containing a ten foot length of inch and a half diameter rubber shock cord and a note saying "Good fishing. Al." Where on earth they had managed to find rubber shock cord Forbush could not tell but he remembered that one American Antarctic station had been supplied with snakebite antidote, shark repellant, and obstetrical forceps and ceased worrying.

The penguin chicks were forming their crèches rapidly. There was not much time. He spent an excited half hour in the rookery watching them. There was little indication now of the old colony divisions, for the chicks had gathered in clusters which combined the populations of several colonies. As far as he could tell the few adult penguins scattered among them were not acting as guardians yet they occasionally rallied to hiss at skuas which alighted too close. Some of the chicks were already starting to lose the thick down which made them look like tiny children in floppy grey pyjamas as they scuttled together back and forth over the rookery rocks responding in a mass to the cries of any parent which came from the ice calling its chicks to feed. It was apparent that chicks and parents recognised each other by their call notes but often hungry chicks would pursue the wrong parent, running too fast for their stubbly legs, calling plaintively and falling over. The parents never gave food within the circle of the crèche but always forced the chicks to act out the ritual of the feeding chase even though this made them more vulnerable to the skua's attacks. A few yards from the crèche the pestered parent would stop, open its beak and regurgitate food into the straining and thrusting open beak of the chick. Forbush saw three chicks knocked down by skuas in flight as they struggled to regain the safety of the crèche after failing in a feeding chase. The skuas pounced with low swoops knocking the chicks off their feet and then dragging them with their beaks to a quieter place where they could batter them to death on the stones. Sometimes a chick could beat off an attack and fight its way back to the crèche. Sometimes a pair of skuas helped each other to strip the living flesh from a chick which would die slowly and still struggling. Forbush was enraged. He ran away over the scoria slopes to set up his catapult, the hot and ammoniac guano dust of the rookery stinging in his nostrils.

He worked with great care and precision, lashing two equal lengths of shock cord to the catapult arms and then making them fast to the reindeer skin boulder sling. He selected a smooth oval piece of lava and fastened it in the sling with two pieces of balloon cord which in turn were made fast to the spliced winch rope so that when the balloon cord was cut the stone would be held in the sling by its forward thrust and released at the peak of its acceleration. With care he cranked back the winch, tightening the rubber, fearful that he might have misjudged the length so that either the strain on the arms was great enough to break them or the rubber would give insufficient power to the missile. He took out his knife and hardly dared cut.

More than a hundred skuas were on the lake. There was no wind to deflect the shot. The evening was clear and calm. The sun was high and behind him so that his targets were clearly defined and he was shooting out of the sun's glow. The mountain was perfectly reflected in the lake except when its smoke plume was made to boil up by the ripple of a swimming skua. He heard their harsh cries and crowing, waiting impatient for a cluster of birds to come into his sighting line and estimated range. Would the boulder be too heavy? Would the recoil lift the catapult from its base? He noted that the nylon rope and balloon cord had stretched sufficiently to take the edge of tension off the rubber, and took another turn on the winch, crouched behind the base beam squinting along the sightline with his sharp knife ready to snip the restraining cord. Now. The boulder sailed one hundred and fifty yards clear over the populated part of the lake passing close to one flying skua so that it checked and squawked but dropping with a mighty splash in unruffled water. Inflamed with success Forbush, with shining eyes and shaking hands, sought another boulder. Should he choose a heavier missile or decrease the power of the propelling charge? Overcome with visions of glorious victory, crushing defeat of the enemy Forbush chose a larger boulder. He wasted no time and fumbled not a moment in making the missile fast, winching back to the fullest stretch of the rubber. "Ha ha. I'm cool as a cucumber. I've got the upper hand. Fire!" His knife slashed, the boulder sailed to the lake edge and appeared to knock over a preening skua. When it took to flight he was sure he had inflicted damage. "I got it. It's groggy. I'll fix the bastards."

The next shot fell in the middle of a group of swimming

birds which all took to flight. Forbush was enraged and for five angry minutes sought a boulder of precisely the right size and weight. With this he scored, knocking back into the water a bird just taking flight. Three shots later he hit one of the concourse of birds which now wheeled in shrill alarm about their roost. It fell as lifeless as his stone into the lake.

"Ai ai ai. I'm a genius." He danced and capered, a grotesque and abandoned figure shouting to the sun and smoking mountain beside his hideous machine of death and quite unaware that the ice was moving in the Sound, that the giant floes were splitting and parting under the relentless pressure of the northward flowing sea, that they were now floating majestically, groaning in their release each time a crack was closed tight by the turning pressure of the current, flowing northwards and away for ever. The two skuas floated dead in the still lake under a high-wheeling cloud of their calling companions.

"Oh lord the sea. The sea is coming!"

Forbush began to run down the slope, twisting and turning among the lava pinnacles, sliding on the scoria pebbles, falling and gashing the palm of his right hand on a sharp outcrop as he scrambled forward still moving and stumbling to his feet all in one motion towards the lake, past the two dead skua gulls rocked now by a faint ripple of wind, round the edge of the lake across the seaward bank to the cliff top. His polar cap had flapped off his head. Blood dripped down his hand on to the stones. He stood with his mouth open, staring seawards at the stately and deliberate movement of the ice. It was as if the floes acted with mind and power, waiting calm and orderly until it was their turn to move and then quietly sailing out into the northward flow. As soon as there was clear water at the fast iceedge another piece would break off and begin its own journey.

The sea was clear just south of Horseshoe Bay a mile away. In half an hour it was clear to the beach below Forbush. Half an hour later a big floe just north of the Cape detached itself and began to move very slowly out from the land, to revolve as if it would roll like a giant wheel clear up the coast of Ross Island into the open sea. Forbush stood and watched the sea, not noticing the passing of time or the movement of the sun, heedless of the wheeling skuas and not hearing their cries.

The world was crumbling around him. The old, still and familiar landscape was floating away, the ice hummock off Access Beach, even the stranded growler had responded to some unseen tremor of the tide and now paraded past him as if he should salute and wish it fair weather and a fast melt. The water between each floe was so deeply blue, the ice beneath the water the purest emerald. The sun was reflected in the sea below him not as a broad shining pathway but as a single golden sphere like a burnished plate on the sheerest deep blue satin. He could reach down and pluck it out of the sea.

He felt as if he had never really believed that the sea would come and the Cape be freed, as if he had been warned of freedom in a dream, discarded its truth and now was shocked by its reality. Twenty feet beneath him he could see into the water, see the stones lying on the shelving bottom, see the very edge of the sea against the stones of the beach, completely calm of surface yet seeming to shiver and move slightly as if it was breathing, tensing its limbs to shake off the aching burden of the ice. There was no life. The stones above and below the water edge were smooth and unmarked, clean and sterile with the grinding of the ice. There was no life, no clustered shells or clotted weeds.

It was midnight. Forbush scrambled back around the cliffs to Access Beach loath to leave sight of the marvellous sea. At the south end of the beach where the ice was now breaking away in smaller pieces groups of penguins were standing on the seaward edge and riding with each floe to the other end of the beach where they dived off into the water swimming at full speed for the beach, broaching like porpoises every few yards, scrambling up among the boulders and ice blocks along the shore and returning to ride the next floe. The night was loud with their harsh and excited call notes. Forbush sat on the cliff above the beach admiring their powerful swimming, straight as spear-thrusts, longing himself to swim, longing for the sound of surf on the beach, the sound of wind-broken water.

Far out in the Sound he could see a school of killer whales, their high sickle fins gleaming in the sun, their breath condensing in clouds like shell-bursts. A skua gull was fishing, diving from height like a gannet but stopping its fall with powerful wing-beats so that only its head and shoulders entered the water before it thrust again in forward flight. Three seals swam into the beach diving and twisting about each other with fluid strength as they came, and hauling themselves on to the stones with ungainly humping of their backs.

"O sea, the sea. How long you took to come. How very, very long."

CHAPTER ELEVEN

FORBUSH sat on his throne. With his binoculars he watched a sea leopard scramble on to an ice-floe and find blood lying in the depression left by a resting Weddell seal. The sea leopard's nostrils flared and its big head swung from side to side. It rubbed its nose in the blood until its head was stained deep red with a mixture of blood and snow crystals and there were crimson splashes on its pale tawny breast and shoulder fur. The seal lay on the surface of the water two hundred yards off Access Beach with blood oozing from a gash in its stomach. Perhaps it has escaped from a killer whale, Forbush thought.

He saw that if the seal tried to dive it would die. It lay on the surface of the unrippled blue sea raising its head to breathe with a noisy exhalation of blood and air through its oval nostrils, pinching its nostrils tight shut again and lowering its head to look into the surrounding water. If the seal dived it would die because the great blood vessel in its stomach cavity was ruptured. This was the vessel that functioned like a non-return valve, storing blood which had passed through the seal's lungs, pumped through its heart and circulated round its body giving up oxygen to its muscles, and holding the blood until the dive was over and its lungs re-filled with air. The blood vessel allowed the seal to dive and dive until all its blood was used up and then released the blood to begin the cycle again.

The sea leopard entered the sea without making a ripple and swam fast, a little faster even than a penguin, towards the seal, which dived. The sea leopard followed it. When the sea leopard returned to the surface alone Forbush knew that the seal was dead. The seal took a long time to float up but until it did the sea leopard caught penguins.

Forbush sat on his throne. The water was so still and clear that he could see the sea leopard diving and twisting and playing with the penguin carcasses one by one as it caught them by being able to swim just a little faster.

He watched it toss them into the air and snap at them as they fell. Then it seized them by the skin in its long sharp teeth and shook them again and again until the skin peeled off, until they were largely bare of skin and feathers. Then it ate them. The living penguins stood on Access Beach and said *Aaark* to each other in loud alarmed voices and would not enter the sea.

While he watched the sea leopard his thought dwelt on the destruction of the seal. In an almost mechanical fashion he reviewed this incident over and over again.

He had seen the seal and the water stained with its blood. He had seen the sea leopard with great rocking head and body fully ten feet long crawl up on to the ice-floe after the seal had left it. He had seen the sea leopard lying on the floe and the seal lying in the water. At the same time he had watched the penguins swimming in the water below his cliff and feeding on the krill, which was so thick the sea was stained orange in patches and almost all the penguins had to do to catch it was to swim along with open mouths. He had felt very happy for the penguins and their gluttony (they would eat so much while swimming that they would be sick in the water and begin all over again) but the sea leopard had slipped into the sea without a ripple and the seal had dived.

With his binoculars he now watched the sea leopard swallow its third penguin whole and then swim quietly to lie beside a small block of still fast ice at the south end of the beach with only the top of its head out of the water.

Presently a group of about thirty penguins jumped into the sea and began porpoising and krill fishing in tight formation. Forbush stood up to shout a warning but could say nothing. The sea leopard sped towards them. They scattered immediately, all swimming in different directions, but the sea leopard picked its mark and swam in pursuit, just a little faster than the penguin, between it and the shore. The penguin began to twist and turn but the sea leopard kept behind and closed the distance. The penguin began to swim in rapid circles about twelve feet across but the sea leopard followed it round and round in a wider circle. The penguin became exhausted and slowed down. The sea leopard caught it with a lunge of sharp teeth, tossed it in the air and began to shake the carcass from its skin. Then it ate the penguin as the seal carcass drifted up not fifty yards from the beach.

The sea leopard swam slowly towards the seal carcass, gripped it by the neck and began to worry it. A strip of flesh and two-inch-thick yellow blubber began to come away and the sea leopard, taking a stronger grip, tore the strip away down the seal's chest. Then it tore a second strip from the shoulder to the belly and all the gallons of blood from the seal's big stomach vessel poured into the sea like ink from a cuttlefish, hiding the sea leopard.

The rending of flesh from the seal continued for half an hour. One hundred and fifteen skua gulls gathered at this feast picking small pieces of flesh and blubber and dangling stomach organs from the water without getting their feathers wet and making no sound except for the beating of their wings which Forbush could distinctly hear together with the strong splashing of the sea leopard. After half an hour the sea leopard rested on the surface of the sea for almost an hour beside the carcass, drifting slowly north, and the skua gulls continued feeding without a cry. Then the sea leopard nuzzled the carcass, tore another small slab of flesh from its back and dived. Forbush did not see it again.

The day was 29 January and late in the evening seven penguin chicks without down gathered on Access Beach looking at the water and preparing to depart for the northern sea. Forbush stayed on his throne until they first entered the water, splashed and called to each other for a few minutes and returned to the beach. Four of the chicks returned to their crèches and three, all with numbered bands, remained on the beach.

Late the following morning Forbush walked down to the beach carefully skirting the water of Pony Lake beside Shackleton's rubbish dump, a collection of rusty cans, broken bottles, bleached seal and penguin bones and pieces of the ancient motor-car. The three chicks were gone and a careful search of their crèches failed to reveal them. They were the first of four hundred and ninety-two chicks which would eventually swim north. Forbush felt a sense of accomplishment.

Most of the chicks were now wandering more freely about the rookery, large enough to care for themselves against skua attacks and being fed less frequently by their parents. They were dirty and scruffy with clumps of down clinging over their black and white mature plumage. A few showed no signs yet of shedding down although they were mostly plump and well grown.

While it returned to its crèche from a feeding chase one of these was attacked and knocked down by a skua. The chick stood about ten inches high and weighed about four pounds. When the skua knocked it down it lay wriggling on its back for a few seconds trying to rake the skua with its feet, pecking, beating its flippers, calling in a terrified shrill whistle. It rolled into a muddy pool of guano and melt water, and stumbled to its feet with matted, dripping down to face the skua's next attack which was made, first, front-on with a powerful beak blow followed by violent wing beats which allowed it to kick the chick into the mud again. The chick knocked the skua off its feet with a series of wild flipper blows, and turned to run but was caught again by the downward strike of the skua's feet and rolled down a dusty slope well clear of the crèche. The skua hit it again as it stopped. Then it took the chick by the nape of the neck and worried it, beating its wings to keep balanced. The chick stopped crying. When the skua let go it turned and began to peck hard at the skua's breast under the beating wings. The skua rose two feet into the air, the chick ran and was knocked hard against a rock in its path. Its down was coming out in clumps and there was blood about its head and neck. It whistled once. The skua caught it by the neck again, shaking it, beating it against the stones, barely able to lift it. Blood oozed from holes in the chick's neck. Its flipper beats lost their strength. Five minutes had passed. When the skua let go the chick fell on its back, pecking upwards at the skua's breast, hauling out a few feather tufts. The skua stabbed the chick savagely on the front of the neck and in the eyes. For another four minutes it beat the chick against the stones until it did not peck in return or beat its flippers, but lay on the ground, slowly wriggling its feet. The skua's mate joined in and held the chick's head while the other pecked a hole in its stomach, spitting forth down until the blubbery chest was bared, and then the dark red flesh, which it tore out and ate with head tossed back and quick convulsions of its throat. Then it held the chick by one leg while the other leg still waved slightly and its mate pecked deeper into the chest and stomach, drawing forth entrails, its head and back bathed in blood and the pink milky remains of the chick's last feed. The chick died about this time. The skuas soon left it.

Forbush walked about the rookery for half an hour. The guano stench caught in his nostrils and throat until he was sick beside the shore of Pony Lake. He washed his lips and beard with lake water careful not to drink and trying to swallow the sour taste from his mouth.

For some time he stood looking at his "Polar Penguin Producers" sign, now weathered and faded, leaning forlornly in its cairn of stones. Then he walked across the rookery up the northern slopes among the lava peaks where the skuas roosted. A skua dived at him, shrilly complaining. He saw a slight movement then, yards down the scoria slope in the next gully but could not see what it was that moved. He stood very still while the skua screamed over his head, watching the clump of rocks where he had seen the movement and saw it again. It was the moving, nervous head of a skua chick half dressed in adult plumage, which crouched among the rocks with its wings outstretched, hardly distinguishable from its background. Forbush walked down the slope towards it while the skua screamed. The chick began to creep away down the slope shuffling on spindly legs, balancing upright with the tips of its outstretched wings brushing the stones, darting its head like a small feathered snake. Forbush walked a little faster, the crunch of his mukluks loud on the gravel. The chick began a weaving run into the bottom of the gully and Forbush began to sprint as the skua dived at his head again and again. The chick crouched on the gully floor, motionless again a moment before Forbush grabbed it, holding it pressed against the stones, breathing very heavily with his heart beating hard. He picked up the chick, holding it carefully away from his body until it ejected guano, then bringing it to his chest. He felt its sinewy neck, every vertebra rippling under feathers and down, and felt the beating of its heart on the palm of his hand. He held it so that his left hand firmly encircled its neck with thumb and forefinger and the palm supported its breast, leaving its legs dangling. His right hand closed firmly, folding its wings, and pressed on its back. The skua screamed now from a nearby rock and dived no longer.

He sat on the stones. The sun was hot in the gully and he felt himself sweating under his heavy shirt, even on his forehead where his tanned and snow-blistered skin met the forward line of his tangled hair. His thin body shivered for a few moments and gave way again to heat and nausea. The chick twitched its head nervously, yawned, opening its black beak to show the splendid cruel curve of it. It glanced at Forbush with hard black eyes and then stared forward swallowing so that he could feel the skinny neck bones ripple in his hand. The skua sat silent on its rock and they were quite alone in the windless bottom of the gully. He could see the top of the smoking mountain and longed to ascend its peak.

"Don't be like this, Forbush. It's too hopeless. Too tragic."

When he was ten his father gave him a book about anatomy because he was quite sure he wanted to be a doctor. He could not pronounce the Latin names properly and asked endless questions. In a thicket at the bottom of the garden he found a long-dead cat. One day when his mother gave him permission to light a little fire and pretend he was camping he boiled the carcass and boiled it until the last shreds of flesh came off all the bones. Then he dried the bones in the sun and learned most of their names by studying his anatomy book. He was drunk with knowledge and amazed everyone. His father was very proud of him and gave him a book on physiology.

Love, you said, is like
The flourishing of flowers
In the heart, unnourished
Except by their own radiance

She means, I suppose, that love is giving, only, that the heart is sufficiently blessed by giving to remain whole and purposeful, untrammelled. Why must I always despair because I cannot act?

After the cat business he wanted to become a farmer, mainly, he remembered, because ripe wheat in a paddock smelled so good. Then he began to love the sea and the things that grew in it. Then it was the mountains. When he started to go into the bush and up into the tussock country, up above the snow line, he was overwhelmed with aspiration. Once he had collected moths and butterflies, pinning them by name to cardboard sheets. Their wings dried out, broke and crumbled. He was revolted. But he had to know. Always he had loved animals, birds, wild things. He had never wanted to fight back at them. The chick stirred in his hand, ruffled its wing feathers under his restraining palm and settled again.

"It's too tragic . . . hopeless."

What is? What's the answer? There's no answer. But if I do nothing I'm being used. I'm a victim. There's no answer. If I kill this chick there is no answer. If I let it go there is no answer. If the chick is dead nothing will be changed. If the chick lives nothing will be changed. If I kill this chick I will take nothing away from the world. If I let it go I will contribute nothing to the world.

Wind hurried among the rocks of the Cape. A gust whipped grit off the gully ridge top and it stung Forbush on the face. He heard the single loud clap of a wave breaking on Access Beach.

If all the penguins died and were eaten by all the sea leopards, nothing would change. If no skua gull ever nested on the Cape again, nothing would change. Life is not an individual thing but a total thing, a volume like the sea. Therefore I am a victim. But if I know I am a victim I am a victim no longer. I am free.

He shouted. The voice broke forth from his heart.

"I am free. I'm free. I am. I am free. I do not understand but I am free."

The Cape was silent.

He placed the skua chick carefully on the ground between his feet. It sprawled among the stones with its wings stretched wide in an attitude of self-protection, twisted its ungainly neck and stared at him with hard eyes.

"You. You're a victim, you poor chick." He nudged it with his foot and laughed when it regurgitated pieces of fish and penguin flesh on to his mukluk toe in a sudden spasm of fright. The skuas were victims. The penguins were victims. The sea leopards were victims and the Weddell seals and Ross seals and crab-eater seals and elephant seals and killer whales, the lichens on the rocks, the algae in Pony Lake which managed their desperate life-cycle through freeze and thaw were all victims, and human beings were free only if they knew. Not that they wanted to lord it over the animals. They only wanted to understand. They only wanted to live fruitful understanding lives, creating something. He thought of the two dead skua gulls floating with their feet up and their shattered wings dangling in Coast Lake. To have done that was so negative. It was anti—anti something he did not know about.

The skua chick began to creep away, very slowly at first, with its trailing wing feathers making a small scraping noise on the gravel, and then running quite fast and wheeling up the gully, up the hill to its nest scoop.

The skua on the rock began to crow, wings thrown up and back, chest thrust out with a glorious trumpeted assertion of life. To Forbush it was the sound of affirmation.

CHAPTER TWELVE

In February the days grew colder. Southerly winds whitened the sea. For five days the sky was overcast with fog and snow from the north but little wind. The half-fledged chicks grew wet and miserable. Forbush watched the passage of ships up and down the ice-free Sound and the flight of aircraft making their last trips back and forth from New Zealand before the winter. He began to feel a vague excitement about going home but remained calm until the very end. In a way he did not want to leave and felt, as each group of grown chicks left for the sea swimming boldly north round the headland of Access Beach, that part of his own growth went with them. Several hundred adult birds stood about in the rookery unhappy in moult.

He learned from Scott Base that the last flight home would be on 3 March and waited anxiously for the last chick to leave the rookery in time for him to board it. The skua gulls were going through a final period of courtship and scoop building, perhaps making assertions of fidelity that would last through the long darkness of their separate winters until the time came to breed and lay again.

On the evening of 1 March the last five chicks gathered together on Access Beach. High on his throne he sat, shivering in a whiteout, waiting for them to go. At midnight it was so dark he could hardly see them, but heard their bickering and squawking at the water's edge. He must have dozed, because at four o'clock in the morning when it was again light with the sky clearing from the south, they had gone.

The rookery was silent. A few dozen moulting birds scratched among the stones as he walked back to Shackleton's hut. The skua gulls were teaching their chicks to fly.

After breakfast when he had called Scott Base on the emergency radio schedule and asked to be picked up by helicopter, he finished packing. Al Weiser arrived to collect him at seven o'clock in the evening. All his gear was ready at the helo pad. He had nailed the shutters on the hut windows and secured the doors.

When they took off he saw that the sea was beginning to freeze. There was a slight wind in the Sound and the remnant of an old swell from the north. A plasma of ice crystals was forming on the sea and glowing like soft mother-of-pearl in the low sun. The old sea swell crept under the freezing surface so that it rippled like muscular flesh. The islands were glowing black in the green-black water and blizzard snow piled in clouds about the flanks of Mount Erebus. The sea had the texture of pearl and poured soft flesh, glowing with a misty grey and blue and purple and orange. The sea was feminine and could have been no more sensual. Forbush imagined warmth, a soft embrace. An iceberg drifted in the Sound, through the rippling flesh of the sea, devouring it.